GIRLS *of* MANY LANDS

England ➤ 1592
Isabel: Taking Wing by Annie Dalton

France ➤ 1711
Cécile: Gates of Gold by Mary Casanova

China ➤ 1857
Spring Pearl: The Last Flower by Laurence Yep

Yup'ik Alaska ➤ 1890
Minuk: Ashes in the Pathway by Kirkpatrick Hill

India ➤ 1939
Neela: Victory Song by Chitra Banerjee Divakaruni

Isabel TAKING WING

by Annie Dalton

American Girl®

Visit our Web site at **americangirl.com**

Printed in China.
02 03 04 05 06 07 08 C&C 10 9 8 7 6 5 4 3 2 1

Girls of Many Lands™, Isabel™, and American Girl®
are trademarks of Pleasant Company.

PERMISSIONS & PICTURE CREDITS
The following individuals and organizations have generously given
permission to reprint illustrations contained in "Then and Now":
p. 173—by permission of The British Library, London,
MAPS.162.o.1 f det (*Panorama of London* detail); pp. 174–175—
The Royal Collection, Windsor, Berkshire, U.K., Her Majesty
Queen Elizabeth II (Elizabeth I as a girl); Dover Books (farthingales);
pp. 176–177—The National Trust Photographic Library/Derrick E.
Witty, London (*Sir Thomas Lucy Family*); by permission of
The British Library, MAPS.162.o.1 f det (*Panorama of London* detail);
Bettmann/CORBIS (doctor in plague mask); pp. 178–179—North
Wind Picture Archives (play); © Reflections Photolibrary/CORBIS
(English schoolgirls); AP/Wide World Photos (Queen Elizabeth II).

Illustration by Mark Elliott

**Cataloging-in-Publication Data available from
the Library of Congress.**

To my new granddaughter, Sophie Beatrice,
who was born while this story was being written

Contents

1 A Kindred Spirit

I shot upright in the dark like a swimmer bursting out of a pond. Something had happened while I slept. I could feel a delicious excitement in the air.

I pulled back the bed curtain. Each tiny windowpane had a dull sheen of ice. Outside, feathery shapes drifted against the glass. But it wasn't the first snow that had pulled me out of my dreams. It was the bells ringing from every steeple. It was Christmas Eve.

Every Yuletide since I could walk and talk, I had awakened with the same jolt of joy. Alice, my nurse, would gasp as I dived into her bed, my cold little feet colliding with her warm flesh.

"Go back to sleep," she'd grumble. "Christmas will come soon enough without your tormenting."

I'd be in an agony of impatience. How could anyone

sleep with this shivery bright happiness filling the house! I would never be like that, when I was grown.

But this year for the first time, I lay down again beside my sister Sabine and pulled the covers up over my head. This year and for all future Christmases, my family would never be the same. One by one, we were all drifting away. My mother had been the first.

I would never again see her smiling face, never hear her sing "Lullay My Liking" slightly off-key. And without my mother's presence, nothing felt quite real, including me. I pictured us all frantically filling that empty space, laughing too much, talking too loudly. Aunt Elinor would criticize my table manners. My father would abruptly take himself off to his study. And Sabine would scurry around like a little squirrel, fussing about the table linen, desperately wanting everything to be perfect.

Someone coughed close to my ear—a tiny grating cough. *That isn't Sabine*, I thought in surprise. I lifted a corner of the coverlet and found my baby sister Hope nestling there, fast asleep. Under her frilly nightcap, her little face was flushed with fever.

I vaguely remembered waking in the night to hear her cries. Sabine must have brought her into our bed to soothe her. Now, without a wink of sleep, Sabine had risen to supervise preparations for Christmas Eve.

I flopped down in the high-curtained bed, making it rock and sway like a ship at sea. And I remembered how my brother and sister and I used to hide here behind the curtains, eating stolen gingerbread and whispering secrets in the dark. Now my brother, Robert, was apprenticed to my father's friend, Master Johnson, and was permitted to come home only on feast days and holy days. And Sabine was too busy pretending to be a housewife to spare time for me. She bustled about with my mother's keys jingling at her waist, just as if she were a real grown-up lady and not a girl of barely fifteen. All she talked about was mending or polishing, or some new cure the apothecary had recommended for Hope's perpetual cough.

I glanced at Hope and suppressed a shudder. As usual she had fallen asleep with her eyes open, and the sight of their upturned whites glimmering in the dark made me feel queasy. I loved my little sister but I was sometimes scared to look at her. With her large solemn eyes and the prominent blue vein standing out on her forehead, she hardly seemed to belong to this world at all.

Our cook, Joan, was always saying that my sister was only lent to us. She said that soon the angels would gather Hope up in their arms and take her to be with our lady mother in Heaven.

This made Alice furious. She declared that my baby sister would grow up to have ten huge, strapping sons and live to be a grouchy old lady of a hundred and four. Alice said she knew this for a fact because she had the gift of clear sight from her old Granny Partlet.

A doubting voice reminded me that Alice had not foreseen my mother dying from childbed fever. Our mother did not die at once, but lingered for months, growing weaker and more transparent, floating a little further away from us each day. My father reassured us that she would recover when the mild weather came again. But on the first real day of spring, my mother left this world forever. When they gave me the news, I ran out into the garden and stayed there for hours, afraid to go back indoors.

The ceaseless roar of the city had gone on all around me: the cries of street sellers, the rumble of wooden wheels, clattering hooves on cobbles, and the *clang-clang* of church bells. Birds darted in and out of the thatch, building nests. Celandines and aconites opened glossy new petals to the sun. Everything went on as usual, as if it were just another ordinary day.

Aunt Elinor came to find me, as it was growing dark. She told me I must be grateful because I'd had my mother's love for twelve whole years. "You must be brave, child," she announced. "You must be brave for your father and poor motherless little Hope."

I watched her thin lips shaping the words, but I couldn't seem to grasp what she was telling me. "As your father's eldest daughter, Sabine is the lady of the household now," my aunt said stiffly, as if she resented this. "But I will be by her side, like a second mother, guiding all you children to do your duty."

I felt myself fuming angrily all over again at the memory. My little sister coughed her harsh, grating cough and mumbled in some private baby language.

A tiny feather had settled on her lip, rising and falling with her breath. I was just going to remove it when I heard footsteps outside the door. Meg, our new maid, came in, carrying a jug in one hand and a flickering candle in the other.

"Merry Christmas, Meg!" I kept my voice soft so as not to startle my little sister in her sleep. Meg shyly returned my greeting.

I slid out from under the covers, and the cold struck me like an icy wave. I took the jug and poured the water into a basin, talking through chattering teeth. "Have you been out in the snow? I love the first snowfall, don't you? I love knowing that no one has trodden there before me, except birds and foxes."

Meg was trying to coax my little sister to wake. "It's morning, little one," she crooned. "Poor Alice has the rheumatiz, so Miss Sabine says I have to get you dressed downstairs in the warm."

Hope gave a sleepy whimper and flung up an arm.

"She'll wake by herself," I told her. "Stay and talk while I wash. Just for a minute."

"Just for a minute then, miss," Meg said.

I was trembling with cold in my linen shift. The water was barely warm, having lost its heat on the way up from the kitchen, but I washed myself bravely with squishy soap, getting the ordeal over with as quickly as possible.

"Aren't you longing for tonight?" I asked Meg through sounds of splashing. "I love Christmas Eve, don't you?"

"I expect I liked it when I was little, miss. Now that I am grown it is just another day."

I felt a shock of surprise. That was exactly how I had been feeling!

"It is better when you're little," I agreed. "Alice used to tell me this beautiful story about how at midnight on Christmas Eve, all the beasts in the land kneel down in their stables to welcome the Christ child. Did your mother used to tell you that story?"

"I don't rightly remember," she said politely.

I sighed with frustration. Meg had started working for us almost six weeks ago. At first I only caught glimpses of her, strewing fresh rushes in the hall and hanging out the washing. She had brown hair and rosy coloring, and I guessed she was about my own age, though not so tall.

Since my mother's death, I had felt not lonely
so much as lost. None of the families we knew had
daughters my own age, and I had begun to long for
a kindred spirit. Meg intrigued me. We had scarcely
spoken, but I sensed that Meg might be the kindred
spirit I'd been wishing for. Our new maid always
looked as if she was on the verge of a smile, and her
humorous brown eyes held a knowing spark. She was
full of life and mischief, just as I used to be. If I could
only get her to stand still long enough to have a
proper conversation, I knew we could be great friends.
I was so sure of this that it never occurred to me Meg
might not feel the same! Yet as the weeks passed, she
seemed to be going out of her way to avoid me. If she
was forced to speak, she was painfully respectful, bobbing a little curtsy, mumbling, "Yes, miss. No, miss."

This morning I decided that I would trick Meg into
talking to me by asking her questions that couldn't be
answered with a "yes" or a "no."

I cleared my throat. "So where do you live, Meg?"
I asked slyly.

"Oh, you would not know it, miss. 'Tis no place for

gentlefolk," she said at once.

My eyes widened. "You mean it is dangerous?"

She gave me her knowing grin. "Not for me, miss. I have been brought up to take care of myself."

I tried again. "Are you the oldest or youngest in your family? Or are you in the middle like me?"

She shrugged. "Mercy, miss, I couldn't say. There's such a crowd in our house, my mother can't keep track."

I was bewildered. "Alice said you had three brothers. She said you told her one brother had just started work at the Rose Playhouse."

But Meg was bending over my little sister, making it impossible to read her expression.

I opened the clothespress and took out my new kirtle. The fine crimson velvet smelled of the lavender flowers Sabine used to keep away moths. I began to tug the gown over my head.

"I've always longed to go to the playhouse," I said in a muffled voice. "Aunt Elinor says that playhouses breed plague and pestilence. But she only says that because I'm a girl. My brother and his friends have seen dozens of plays, and he's as fit as a flea. Have you ever been to a playhouse, Meg?"

I emerged breathlessly and felt myself go red as I realized I had been chattering away to myself. Meg had gone, taking my little sister with her.

I felt a twinge of distress. Perhaps Meg thinks I look down on her for being a servant. Maybe she thinks I believe myself to be very high and mighty. She doesn't realize I just want to be friends. *But that's terrible*, I thought. *I must do something.*

Then and there, I decided to show Meg she was wrong. I would go down to the kitchen and help her wash my sister, just as if we were equals!

I ran downstairs, my new leather shoes slipping and sliding on the polished wood. The hall was decked with festive garlands of evergreen, holly, mistletoe, and bay. Their woody fragrance mingled with the rich smells of simmering fruits and spices from the kitchen. Joan had been cooking for days. Now the larder was crammed with good things to eat. Unfortunately, I arrived in the kitchen just as Joan was scolding Meg for burning the frumenty, the special wheat porridge my father loved.

Joan interrupted her tirade to turn and remove a bubbling kettle from the fire. Quick as lightning, Meg pulled a hideous face. Then she saw me in the doorway, and gave a little gasp. I grinned at her from behind Joan's big broad back and pretended to lock my lips, to reassure Meg that I wouldn't tell.

"May I help Meg bathe my sister?" I asked Joan in my most innocent voice.

"That's not for me to say, little mistress," she said disapprovingly. "But you had better not make a mess of my nice clean floor."

I had hoped Meg and I would be able to talk at last, but that proved impossible. Joan seemed to be deliberately crashing pots and pans like some vengeful kitchen goddess. Meg gave me a humorous look, and I tried hard not to laugh.

Meg emptied the steaming kettle into the tub, carefully adding cold water until the bathwater was comfortably warm. I undressed my solemn-eyed baby sister. We quickly lifted her into the warm bath and began to soap her waxy, pale limbs. Hope was never sure if she liked being bathed. An anxious expression came into her eyes, and her bottom lip quivered.

I sang "Ride a Cockhorse," her favorite rhyme, gently splashing my sister's tummy in time to my singing. Then Meg began to sing a song I had heard sung in the street, "Bonny Sweet Robin Is All My Joy." I joined in and felt my spirits soar. It made me ridiculously happy to hear our two voices singing the same melody, and I think Meg felt the same. My baby sister clapped her hands with pleasure. As soon as the song was over, she made hopeful little singing sounds, wanting us to sing it again.

"This bath is taking a long time," Joan said suspiciously. "If that baby were made of sugar she'd have melted by now." She turned her back on us and began furiously grating nutmeg for a delicious sweet custard she called a *doucet*.

I decided to seize my chance. I put my head close to Meg's and whispered, "I'm glad you came to work at our house. Maybe we could go for a walk one day, when you've finished your work?"

Meg regarded me thoughtfully. Then she broke into a shy smile and whispered, "I should like that, miss."

Hope had realized she was no longer the center of attention. She made a loud crowing sound, to make us notice her, and whacked the bathwater with both hands. Big soapy waves sloshed out over the floor. My sister was delighted. "Oh, oh, OH!" she sang out.

Joan swung round to see what was going on and saw Meg hastily mopping up the puddle. "Dry that poor mite and get her dressed before she catches her death!" she ordered.

Aunt Elinor appeared in the doorway. "What are you thinking of, Isabel!" she sniffed. "The servants have work to do. You really must not get under their feet in this way!"

"Yes, Aunt Elinor. Sorry, Aunt Elinor," I said meekly, and I hurried out of the kitchen before my aunt could think of some new reason to scold me.

2 "Lullay My Liking"

I had always sensed that I was a great disappointment to Aunt Elinor.

Everything I did seemed to annoy her. I read poetry when I should be plying my needle, made up long, enthralling stories in my head when I was meant to be studying household accounts, and ran about the streets like an urchin when I was supposed to glide silently from place to place like a swan.

My aunt insisted that she simply wished to discipline me, as my own mother would have done. But my mother never once sniffed at me as if I were a herring that had gone bad, nor did she tell me I must try to be a lady like Sabine. Yet Aunt Elinor did both these things several times a day.

I went into the parlor where Meg had set out cold

meats, cheese, and home-baked bread to break our fast, with a small jug of beer to wash it down. My father sat alone at the table, gazing out at the falling snow. His bread and cheese lay uneaten on his platter. He looked tired and strained, as if he had not slept well. I guessed that he, too, had lain awake, remembering happier Christmases.

My father suddenly registered my presence, and his face lit up. "Merry Christmas, poppet!" He kissed me, and I felt his beard prickle my cheek.

I knelt to receive my father's blessing, as I did at the start and close of every day. "Merry Christmas, sir."

When I was a little girl, I used to think all fathers smelled of nutmeg and cinnamon. My father was a merchant trading in spices. His work often took him away from home for months at a time. Once when I was small, he sailed away to the Indies and was gone for over a year.

He held me at arm's length, and I saw that his expression was wistful. "You are wearing your new kirtle, Isabel. It makes you look even more like your mother than ever."

I was the only one of his children who resembled our mother, and I knew this made me doubly precious. When my aunt complained about my unladylike behavior, my father just said, "Let my little kitten have her fancies. She will be grown soon enough." I had come to take his indulgence for granted. Yet I felt somehow cheated. My father was humoring me like a favorite pet, and I wanted him to take me seriously.

He sensed the change in my mood. "What ails you, sweeting?"

"Nothing, sir. I am impatient to see my brother, that's all," I invented quickly. "He will not return home for hours yet."

My father smiled. "You two were always great play-mates. What was that game you played all the time?"

I laughed. "We called it 'Samarkand.' We had no idea where this magical country was. We just thought it sounded exciting and romantic!"

He let out a roar of laughter. "I seem to remember that your mother's best silk wrap mysteriously went missing whenever you played that game. Not to mention a lot of spices from the kitchen."

"Those were our goods," I told him merrily. "We sailed over the high seas to Samarkand in a fine sailing vessel. We used our nurse's bed for this part of the game, because it pitched about so realistically, like a ship in a storm. Then when we reached the shores of the mysterious Orient at last, we traveled along the Silk Road by pack mule, braving dangers to bring back silks and spices for Her Royal Grace, the queen!"

My father shook his head, still smiling. "You were such an adventurous little girl. Remember how you insisted that Robert read to you every night from that old book of travelers' tales, even though it gave you such nightmares!" He sighed. "You must miss him, especially now that . . ." His voice trailed off.

"I do," I said softly. "I miss him every single day."

"Why not go to meet the young rascal?" he suggested unexpectedly. "'Tis Christmas Eve. Master Johnson will be sure to let his apprentices go early."

"Oh, thank you," I breathed. I could hardly believe it. I would have my beloved brother all to myself!

My father's voice became teasing. "Perhaps, by the time she gets home again, my little chatterbox will have talked herself hoarse and the rest of us will get a word in edgeways!"

After I had eaten my bread and cheese, I ran to look for my old nurse. I found her in a quiet corner of the kitchen with a basket of darning. I noticed she sat stiffly, as if she was still in pain. I knelt beside her. "You are not well, Alice," I said anxiously.

"Hush, 'tis just the cold in my bones. I'll mend by and by," she chuckled. "But now you're here, you can thread this needle for me."

I dropped my voice, making sure no one could hear me. "Alice, I want to buy a Christmas present for Meg. What do you think she would like?"

"I think you should leave her alone," she advised. "Meg can't go making friends with you, child."

"Why not?" I said in dismay.

"You know why not. Your father sees fit to educate you, even though you are but a girl. Meg is a poor working girl who cannot read or write."

"That's a horrible thing to say," I burst out. "I do not care if Meg is poor."

"But it may be that Meg cares, my honey," my nurse said gently.

"Please, Alice," I wheedled. "Please. It is Christmas. I know my lady mother gave you little gifts at Christmastime."

Her old wrinkled face softened. "That she did. I have those fine leather gloves she gave me still."

There was a jingle of keys, and Sabine bustled in looking as neat and trim as always in her blue dress and crisp white cap. Aunt Elinor insisted that my sister was the image of herself when she was a girl, but I could not believe my tight-lipped aunt had ever been so pretty.

Sabine pinched my cheek affectionately. "Our father tells me that you are running off to the docks, Isabel."

I noticed dark circles under her eyes and felt a twinge of guilt. "I don't have to. I'll stay and help you if you really need me to," I said earnestly.

She tucked a stray curl back under my cap. "No, you go, poppet. We all know how you have been missing Robert."

My eyes prickled with tears. She sounded just like the old Sabine, the sweet-natured sister who sat up with me all night, telling stories, when I had the chicken pox and couldn't sleep for itching. She was but nine years old then, three years younger than I was now. Sometimes I got the feeling Sabine had actually been born grown up.

"I'll help you when I get back," I promised. "I'll do anything you ask."

She laughed. "Thank you, Isabel, dear! You can drag in the Yule log!"

"Anything sensible, you zany!" I giggled. We both knew it would take at least two strong men to carry out that particular Christmas task. The Yule log was chosen for its great size, so that it would burn steadily throughout the twelve days of Christmas and bring the household good fortune throughout the coming year.

After our noon meal, I dressed warmly in stout boots and my woolen cloak with the fur trim. It was a long walk to Robert's workplace, four miles or more.

"Don't forget to use your pomander," my aunt called after me. "It is of no use dangling from your belt like an ornament."

I held my pomander to my nose, inhaling the strong spices, then reeled back dramatically like an actor in a play. "Like that, you mean, aunt?" I called teasingly.

"Impertinent child," she sniffed. "Contagion is no laughing matter."

My aunt was always fretting about us catching the plague. When she was a girl, thousands of people had lost their lives in a terrible epidemic. Since then she had lived in perpetual dread of its return, though no cases had been reported for years now.

I shut the door behind me, pulling a face. If it had been up to my aunt, I would never have been allowed out of the house! Pulling my cloak closely around me, I set off along the cobbled streets, my boots crunching on the powdery snow and my warm breath flying ahead of me in frosty plumes.

The sun had come out, and the pale wintry light had turned London's Cheapside into a kingdom in a fairy tale. Every roof and steeple, every stone saint and gargoyle sparkled with freshly fallen snow. Even the piles of frozen rubbish in the streets were softly quilted with white.

Cheapside was always a bustling place, but today I felt as if I were wandering through a magical winter fair. Clowns and jugglers, street sellers and musicians all competed for the coins of passersby.

An awed crowd had formed in front of the lace maker's. I caught the flicker of flames against the snow and heard a sudden collective gasp. I ran over to see what was going on and saw a hairy giant of a man brandishing a blazing torch. He looked exactly like a devil I had seen on a stained-glass window. His long hair was matted with filth, his breeches were torn, and despite the freezing weather, his chest was bare. I watched in mixed horror and amazement as the giant arched his back and plunged the torch again and again into his open mouth, appearing to swallow the flames.

People stamped and cheered, and a hail of coins rattled into his cap. But one old woman made the sign of the evil eye as if she was afraid.

I tossed a silver farthing into the fire-eater's greasy cap, then hurried away. I still had Meg's present to find. I had passed dozens of stalls selling trinkets and festive things to eat: roasted apples, their skins glossy with honey; iced gingerbread in the shape of stars. But I wanted something special.

At last I spotted a man with a tray hanging around his neck, selling a whole menagerie of sugar animals. I bought a pink mother pig with a litter of tiny pink piglets, and he wrapped them carefully in golden tissue. *Everyone loves sugar,* I told myself happily. *Even Queen Elizabeth!*

Delighted with myself, I hurried on through a maze of crooked streets. A chill wind plucked at my cloak. I was now but a short distance from the river Thames, and from time to time I caught the gray flash of water running past the end of an alleyway. By twists and turns the street took me down to the waterfront, and I felt the familiar prickle of excitement as I recognized the jaunty spires and rooftops of Southwark across the river.

My aunt said Southwark was a wild, lawless place. But her obvious disapproval only made me more eager to explore this forbidden territory for myself. The south bank of the Thames was crowded with play-houses, unsavory taverns, gambling houses, and bear gardens, where people paid to watch half-starved dogs savage an equally starved captive bear. I had no wish to visit the bear gardens, but I longed with all my heart to go to the playhouse. *Meg is lucky*, I thought wistfully. *Her brother works in the theatre. She can see plays every time she has a day off.*

I went on my way past workshops filled with sawing and hammering and the fresh reek of new wood. My toes and fingers were numb by the time I reached Master Johnson's house. I waited impatiently, stamping my boots and breathing the dockland smells of salt, tar, and rope, all mingled with the chilly scent of coming snow. And suddenly there was Robert racing toward me with a sprig of bay in his cap.

"But my little mouse has grown so tall!" he exclaimed.

"Not so tall," I protested. "I am sure I have not grown an inch since you came home last!"

In reply, my brother just swung me off my feet, making me scream with laughter. At last he set me down again. Calling a cheerful "Merry Christmas!" to a fellow apprentice, Robert tucked my arm in his and we started back toward home, laughing and talking.

"How is everyone?" he asked.

"All well, except for Hope, who still has her cough." I sighed. "But everything is so dull without you. I have no interesting news to tell. I would much rather hear about you."

My brother immediately launched into a glowing description of his new life. Just as he had done when he came home at Michaelmas, he managed to bring his master into every other sentence. Master Johnson had done this or Master Johnson had said that.

Robert's legs were still longer than mine, and I had to hurry to keep up. I suddenly pictured myself bounding along at his side like some eager puppy and felt twinges of jealousy. As children playing at being spice traders, my brother and I had been equals. But

Robert was a man now and part of the real world of docks and shipbuilding, buying and selling, as I could never be.

"We'll go this way," he said suddenly. "I want to show you something." My brother seized my hand, pulling me eagerly toward the waterfront.

Usually the docks were filled with seamen in red stocking caps, unloading sacks and barrels and swarming up and down the rigging. But today it seemed eerily deserted. And with their sails furled like buds and their masts and rigging furred with snow, even the ships seemed to be sleeping.

"You did not used to be so quiet, mouse," Robert teased. "What's wrong?"

I tried to smile. "I was just wishing that I were a boy."

He looked amused. "Why do you say that, you funny little creature?"

"Because girls must always be good and stay at home. But when you are a boy, the whole world can be your home. Men build houses and ships and sail off to discover strange new worlds. But women must stay indoors, sewing stitches so fine that no one will ever see them. Our work is only visible if we do it badly."

"I had not thought of it that way," Robert admitted. "But Isabel, I want to—"

I had not meant to pour out my heart, but now that I had begun, I seemed unable to stop. "Aunt Elinor says I must be ladylike, like Sabine. But I will never be like her in a thousand years. Do you know our sister sleeps without ruffling the sheets—"

But Robert had stopped listening. "Isabel, hush!" he interrupted. "We're here!" He pointed across the choppy waters of the dock. "There she is." My brother's voice was filled with wonder.

Dipping and curtsying in front of us was the most beautiful ship I had ever seen. Painted on her side in gold and sapphire letters was her name, *The Rosalind*.

"Isn't she fine?" Robert's face shone.

I felt a sudden lump in my throat. My brother had not brought me to see *The Rosalind* just because she was beautiful.

"She belongs to Master Johnson," he explained.

I tried to swallow, but the lump was still there like a stone.

"Master Johnson says this is a golden age for Englishmen. He says that if we have courage and use the wits God gave us, the wonders of the world will be ours, like apples waiting to be picked."

With a pang, I whispered, "You are going to the Indies, like Father did, aren't you? I had not thought you would go so soon."

Robert put his arm around me. "Not so soon as all that. We will not set sail until after New Year."

I knew this was a wonderful opportunity for Robert, and I struggled to be pleased for him. "You are lucky," I told him bravely. "You will see those strange sights we once read about in our book of travelers' tales, do you remember? Oliphants, and cockodrills, and strange humans whose heads grow under their arms!"

"I am not an explorer, you know, Isabel," he laughed. "I'll be buying spices for Master Johnson, not discovering new lands."

"You don't fool me," I said. "You can't wait to go!"

"No," Robert admitted sheepishly. "I can't."

Our teasing turned into a play fight. He snatched off my hood and I chased after him, laughing. But I think my brother guessed I was still sad, because on the way home he tried to cheer me up with tales of a fearsome pirate queen who sailed the waters of the Americas. "It's true. Ask Master Johnson if you don't believe me. Our own queen greatly admires her," he grinned.

By the time we reached home, we were both pink-cheeked from our long walk in the snow. Robert was scandalized to find that no one had brought in the Yule log and immediately went in search of my father. Grunting with effort, the two of them wrestled the huge log indoors. It looked magical with its ropes of ivy and brightly colored ribbons. When they had dragged the log onto the hearth, my father ceremoniously lit it with a piece of wood that had been saved specially from last year's Yule log.

The flames crackled and gradually took hold. A shower of blue sparks went up the chimney, and my baby sister said, "Pretty, pretty!" These were the first words she had spoken. We all kissed and praised her, and Hope looked astonished, as if she didn't know what all the fuss was about.

My father continued gazing into the fire. "Your

mother always said there was no other wood that smelled as sweet," he said with a contented smile.

"It's true," Robert agreed.

Sabine lit the tall Christmas candles she had bought from the chandler earlier in the week, and suddenly the room was alive with tiny golden flames glinting back from polished wood and pewter and the glossy leaves of evergreen.

And with a shiver of happiness, I understood that Christmas would come again this year as every year. Even without my mother.

Meg had spread a white linen cloth upon the table and set out all our best pewter and the fine Venetian glasses. Now she began to run in and out with steaming dishes, and we sat down to the traditional meal of salt fish, winter greens, and Joan's good bread, followed by a great bowl of golden frumenty, glittering with crystals of sugar. We ate simply on Christmas Eve. The true feasting began tomorrow. Yet of the twelve days of Christmas, this was the one I loved the best, when the whole world held its breath, waiting for the Christ Child to be born.

After the meal, we sat by the fire, roasting chestnuts and drinking mulled wine. Without thinking, I took down my mother's lute and began to sing "Lullay My Liking." Everyone joined in, even Aunt Elinor. Then we sang "The Cherry Tree Carol," which was my father's favorite.

I saw that my little sister was growing drowsy, so I set down the lute and she instantly climbed upon my knee and went to sleep. My father and brother began to sing a merry drinking song. But by this time Sabine and I could scarcely keep our eyes open. We bid the men good night and carried my sleeping sister upstairs. Alice was not yet recovered, so we laid Hope gently in the middle of our bed, undressed quickly to our linen shifts, and dived under the covers, squeaking with shock as our warm skin made contact with the icy sheets.

Sabine kissed my cheek. "Merry Christmas, Isabel," she whispered, and snuffed out the candle.

"Do you think our mother heard us singing?"
I whispered back.

"I'm sure of it, poppet."

For some time I lay awake in the dark, feeling thankful that Christmas Eve had been so much happier than my gloomy imaginings. And imperceptibly, my thoughts turned into a dream.

Robert, Sabine, and I were young children again, playing our favorite game of Samarkand. In my dream, this imaginary journey miraculously became real. It was a sparkling moonlit night, and we were traveling the Silk Road on pack mules, in the company of three silent merchants. The men pointed solemnly to a great star hanging in the night sky like a jewel. I understood without being told that these were the Three Wise Men. And we rode on together across desert sands rippling in the moonlight like folds of luminous silk.

3 Sabine's Secret

The day after Christmas was the traditional day for giving Yuletide gifts. I went to find Meg after she had finished work, and to my delight she agreed to come for a walk. We walked down to the river, and when I was quite sure no one was around, I said shyly, "I bought something for you. I hope you will not be offended." And I put the Christmas present into her hands.

Meg stared down at the little parcel with an awed expression. "You bought this for me?" she whispered.

"'Tis but a trifle. Go on, open it," I told her.

If I had been Meg, I would have torn at the paper in my eagerness to see what was inside, but Meg unwrapped my gift with infinite care, as if the wrapping were almost as precious to her as the contents. When she reached the sweetmeats inside, she gave a gasp of pleasure. "Oh, miss, you shouldn't have! Miss, they've even got little curly tails made of string!" I knew that Meg was genuinely delighted, because she had turned as pink as the sugar pigs!

But the joy of the holidays didn't last. At New Year, Meg went home to visit her family. The following day, her mother sent word that Meg had fallen ill with a quinsy and could not yet return to work. Soon afterward, my brother sailed for the Indies, and the atmosphere in our house changed for the worse.

It seemed to me that Aunt Elinor and Sabine were always behind closed doors talking secrets. If I tried to join them, my aunt shooed me away impatiently. I felt bewildered and left out. I took to roaming the city streets while I made up long, rambling stories in my head. I pretended that I lived in a world where girls could do everything their brothers could do and more. I set off on imaginary adventures and performed fearless heroic feats, and no one ever told me to behave like a lady.

But one day I stayed out in the cold too long and caught a severe chill. After that, I was imprisoned indoors for days, enduring my aunt's and sister's whispers and mysterious glances. Finally my aunt declared me well enough to resume my schooling.

"Your sister and I have enough to do without you moping around, cluttering up the place," she sniffed.

Alice was not so easily convinced and insisted on dosing me with her remedy to be on the safe side. My old nurse moved stiffly as she took the kettle from the hob and poured boiling water onto the herbs in the bowl. The kitchen filled with heady fumes of peppermint, rosemary, and thyme. Alice tossed in a piece of dried root tied in muslin, then made me lean over the bowl. "Breathe deeply, my honey," she commanded, and quickly draped a cloth over my head, creating a stifling tent.

I took a deep breath and choked. "Ugh, Alice, it smells terrible!"

"You want to be well for your tutor tomorrow, don't you?"

"Oh, yes!" I said fervently, and accidentally inhaled so much foul-smelling steam that my nose and eyes began to stream violently.

Eventually, to my relief, Alice announced that all the good physic had evaporated. I kissed her good night. "Sleep well, my honey," she said softly. "All will be well, by and by." I noticed a sad note in her voice, almost as if she pitied me for some reason.

I went out into the drafty corridor, drawing my shawl around my shoulders. Low murmurings came from behind the parlor door, and I scowled to myself. Sabine and Aunt Elinor must be discussing one of those grown-up secrets, which they considered me too young and ignorant to understand.

Sabine came to bed after I had fallen asleep, and the next morning I woke just as she was tiptoeing out of our chamber to see to her household duties. When I went downstairs, I found that my father had risen early to attend to some business at his warehouse, so I had to break my fast alone.

There seemed to be a great deal of activity in the kitchen for so early in the day, busy clatterings and whisking sounds and unusually savory smells coming from the oven. I heard my aunt questioning our cook and I heard Joan answer, "I roasted a sirloin of beef, like Mistress Sabine said, and I am cooking a fine young kid with a pudding in its belly. And there is a great game pie in the larder."

They were obviously planning a feast of some kind, but as today was not a feast day, I could not imagine why. I went slowly back up the stairs. *Master Hart's lessons are all I have to look forward to now*, I thought forlornly.

Outside the schoolroom, I stopped and sniffed the air. Surely that was not wood smoke? Aunt Elinor disapproved of heating schoolrooms on principle, believing that children's brains functioned best in a cold room. I opened the door and was astonished to see Meg crouching in front of the hearth, blowing busily on some kindling. It was her first day back at work since her illness.

"Meg, it does my heart good to see you," I cried. "How strange that we were both ill at the same time! Did my aunt ask you to light a fire for me?"

She looked a little flustered. "Not exactly, miss. Alice said you had been poorly, and I did not want you to come to harm. I'd better go now, miss. We've got so much to do downstairs, and you know how Joan gets!"

But on her way out, Meg became unusually chatty. "I took your little pigs home to share with my brothers, miss. At first my mother would not believe you had given them to me as a present. My little brother Jem refuses to eat his. He says 'tis too pretty. Tom says if Jem does not eat it soon, he will eat it for him!" She laughed merrily, but I detected a strangely sympathetic expression in her eyes.

We heard Joan shouting from downstairs, and Meg fled from the room. I was glad of my friend's return. She did seem a little too bright and breezy, but that was probably because she was not quite used to being my friend.

I went over to the window and breathed on a frozen pane, melting a peephole into the outside world. In the street below, horses breathed out steamy clouds as they trotted over the frosty cobbles, pulling carts heaped with root vegetables, fish, or firewood. People walked quickly, cloaks swirling.

Master Hart came into sight, cramming bread into his mouth as he walked along, his nose buried in a book as usual. He had forgotten to comb his hair again. It stuck out comically in all directions, like the feathers of a baby jackdaw.

As I watched, my absentminded tutor stepped out in front of a cart. I sucked in my breath with dismay. The carter shouted angrily, but Master Hart calmly went on his way, absorbed in his book.

Minutes later he hurried into the schoolroom, blowing on his hands. He beamed with pleasure to see the fire. "Your aunt is too kind. Good morning, Isabel, and a happy New Year. I hope you are feeling better?"

"I am almost recovered, thank you," I said. "Did you have a merry Christmas, Master Hart?"

"Yes, oh yes," he said. "Indeed I did."

My tutor set me a Latin translation to do. While I worked, he took out a leather note-book and began to scribble intently in its pages. He had confided in me that he took this note-book with him everywhere so as to capture his thoughts and ideas before they faded. Master Hart hoped to be a playwright one day. For a long time the only sounds in the room were the crackling of the fire and the faint scratching of our quills.

After he had corrected my translation, we had our music lesson. Master Hart played the lute beautifully. We played "Greensleeves," one of his favorite pieces.

While we were singing, I had a coughing fit and had to stop to catch my breath.

"You said you were recovered," my tutor said sternly. "Or I should not have made you sing."

"I wanted to sing," I croaked. "You have no idea how much I've missed our lessons."

He beamed at me. "I've missed them, too. Did you read the Ovid I sent you?"

"Oh, yes! And his poetry is wonderful, only—"

I hesitated, not liking to insult Master Hart's gift.

"Please go on," he prompted.

That was the thing I loved about my new tutor. Our old tutor, Master Strype, had believed that girls were incapable of rational thought. But Master Hart always seemed genuinely interested in what I had to say.

I took a breath. "It's just that poets always make their heroines meet such unhappy ends."

"So that's your difficulty," he said in a musing voice.

"If a hero dies, it is always in the midst of some thrilling adventure, but a heroine is sure to end by being walled up in a convent or fatally bitten by a snake, or else she simply dies for love, like Dido."

I was overtaken by another fit of coughing. Master Hart waited sympathetically until the bout was over. "Girls in stories do nothing but pine and suffer and seek to be rescued," I managed to gasp out. "Are there no strong, bold heroines, Master Hart?"

"I do know of one," he said, to my surprise. "And if you promise faithfully not to try to speak, I will tell you about her."

I pulled my chair closer to the fire, and Master Hart began to tell me the story of Nicolette, the Saracen slave girl who was so brave and resourceful that she successfully rescued her sweetheart, Aucassin, from the evil lord who had imprisoned him in a tower.

It was midday by the time Master Hart finished his tale, and he had to rush away to tutor some little boys who lived in the next street. I lingered by the fire, warming my hands at the flames. My tutor's tale had both delighted and unsettled me. Was it possible for girls to have adventures after all? Could my wild dreams and imaginings become real?

"Isabel! What do you think you're doing, keeping us waiting like this?"

My aunt frowned at me from the doorway, looking unusually grand in a gown of buttercup yellow. She tsked angrily at my inky hands. "Run and make yourself respectable, child! You are keeping our visitors waiting."

I had not been told we were expecting visitors. But I only murmured, "Yes, Aunt Elinor. Sorry, Aunt Elinor," and ran to my chamber. On the way, I heard a familiar voice booming up from the parlor. *I am sure that is Sir Edmund Glover*, I thought in surprise. *I do hope Henry is with him.*

Henry Glover had been a favorite of mine ever since we visited the Glovers' house in Richmond when I was small. I had embarrassed myself by eating far too much syllabub and becoming ill. Henry had tried to console me by doing conjuring tricks, pretending to find a quail's egg in my ear.

I scrubbed my hands and changed into my new

crimson kirtle and slippers. Then I put on a fresh cap and hurried down to meet our visitors. "Is Henry here—" I began eagerly, then blinked in surprise. The parlor was full of people! Henry was there in a doublet so stiff with gold embroidery that it looked capable of standing up by itself. With him were Sir Edmund and Mistress Glover and half a dozen other Glover relatives, including Sir Edmund's elderly mother. Everyone was dressed as if for some splendid occasion, and Sir Edmund wore the largest ruff I had ever seen.

Hope sat on my aunt's knee in her best kirtle. She was sucking her thumb, looking completely bewildered.

"Come in, poppet!" my father beamed. "Isabel has been studying with her tutor," he explained to everyone proudly.

But no one paid any attention because at that moment, Sabine came into the room behind me. She was wearing a new dress of rose-colored wool, embroidered with tiny flowers, and her hair was swept up under a cap of snowy white lace. She curtsied, and I saw a deep flush spreading along her cheekbones.

"And here is my little Sabine at last," my father said

warmly. He drew my sister to his left side and beckoned Henry to stand at his right, and his voice became strangely formal, as if he was speaking in a church or court of law.

"My wife often spoke of the day our two families would be connected, not only by ties of affection and mutual respect but through the holy sacrament of marriage. This is a very happy and solemn moment."

My father nodded at my sister. Sabine must have rehearsed this moment, for she said haltingly, "I, Sabine Campion, do willingly promise to marry thee, Henry Glover, if God wills and if I live. Until which time, I take thee for my only betrothed husband."

Then Henry announced that he took my sister to be his only betrothed wife, and they shyly exchanged rings. My father made them clasp hands, and they stood there, holding hands and blushing, not knowing what to do next.

"Come, Henry, be not so lukewarm. Kiss your future bride," boomed Sir Edmund. The couple kissed, and everyone roared with laughter.

But I felt numb. My sister and I had shared the same

bed every night since I was four years old, yet Sabine had never once hinted that she was to be betrothed.

"Aren't you going to congratulate the bride-to-be, Isabel?" my aunt sniffed.

"I wish you both a long and happy life," I said dutifully to Sabine. "Does our brother know you are to be married?" I asked her under my breath.

Sabine nodded, still covered in blushes. "We told him before he left."

So it was only me they did not tell.

I remembered the pitying note in Alice's voice as she bade me good night, and the way Meg had acted so flustered when I caught her lighting my fire. Everyone knew! My brother, the servants, everyone in the household knew of Sabine's coming betrothal except for Hope and me, as if we were just two silly little girls who did not count.

I wanted to burst into tears and run from the room. But that would make me look like a spoiled child and shame my father into the bargain. So I forced myself to be the good girl everyone expected me to be. I teased Henry that I had secretly hoped to marry him

myself ever since he had pulled the quail's egg out
of my ear. I told Sabine truthfully that she would be
the most beautiful bride there had ever been. And I
stood beside Aunt Elinor nodding politely as Henry's
grandmother told us a long, involved story about the
time Henry stole and ate a whole marigold tart when
he was but six years old.

I nodded and I smiled, but I felt as if something had
broken inside me.

The celebration went on late into the night.
Eventually I excused myself, saying that I had a
headache. Much later Sabine came softly into our
chamber. She undressed in the dark and climbed into
the bed beside me. "I know you are upset, Isabel," she
whispered anxiously. "I truly wanted to tell you, but I
should have felt so foolish if it had come to nothing,
and Aunt Elinor said—"

I turned over, hunching my back. I could imagine
what Aunt Elinor had said.

Sabine chattered nervously in the dark. "I am so
happy and excited, Isabel. We are to marry in the
spring and there is a great deal to do. I would be so

glad of your help. We used to do everything together, remember?"

A tear slid down my cheek and crawled into my hair. I remembered perfectly. It was Sabine who had forgotten.

She stroked my back softly. "Henry says that when we are married, you can come to stay. He says we will keep a pony for you at our country house, and you can ride it whenever you like. I'm not really leaving you, Isabel."

You're lying, I thought. *Everyone leaves me. First my mother, then Robert, and now you, Sabine. And I'm going to be all alone.*

4 Isabel Steals a Boat

A few weeks after Sabine's betrothal I was in the parlor, watching a few meager snowflakes whirl past the window. It was not the sparkling kind of snow that turns the ordinary world into a fairy tale, but the sharp, stinging kind that comes toward the end of winter, littering sills and gutters like grubby oatmeal. My father had gone to the north of England on business some days ago, leaving my aunt and Sabine in charge of his household.

Suddenly Aunt Elinor stormed in and tossed a letter upon the table. "Your tutor says he has a fever!" she said indignantly. "Master Strype never missed a day's work in all the years he taught you children. 'Twas a great pity the man had to die of the smallpox."

I rose from my chair.

"And where do you think you're going, child?" my aunt demanded.

"To the schoolroom, aunt," I said. "Master Hart gave me a Greek translation to do."

Aunt Elinor gave a scornful laugh. "And how useful do you think Greek and Latin will be when you are married?"

I took a breath. "Perhaps I will not marry," I said daringly.

"What nonsense! All women must marry, you foolish child."

Then my aunt realized what she had said and added hastily, "It was different in my case, for poor Edward died of the sweating sickness but seven days after our betrothal. Your father was kind enough to take me into his home. Not all women are so lucky."

But I didn't think my aunt was lucky to be dependent on her brother's charity. "Can women and girls have nothing in this world unless their male relatives provide it for them?" I asked

My aunt flushed with anger. "You try my patience, Isabel!" she snapped. "It's time you stopped blurting out any nonsense that comes into your head. Your sister will be gone in a few months, and your father will not care a jot for your Greek and Latin then. He will expect his linen starched and his meals on the table and his household to run smoothly."

I felt as if I couldn't breathe. It had never occurred to me that my father would expect me to step into Sabine's shoes and run our household, yet now I realized that it must be so.

"So we shall have no Greek and Latin today," my aunt sniffed. "I will instruct you in more practical matters. We will start with accounts."

I was forced to spend the next hour adding and subtracting tedious columns of figures. Then I followed Aunt Elinor into the scullery and watched dutifully as she demonstrated how to clean grease stains from a velvet doublet with the help of castile soap and a feather.

"A mistress cannot supervise her servants unless she knows how to do their tasks herself," she explained.

"Yes, Aunt Elinor," I said meekly. But when my aunt wasn't looking, I screwed my eyes shut tight and offered up a fervent prayer for Master Hart's speedy recovery.

The days dragged past and my tutor was still too unwell to resume his duties. I was forced to endure Aunt Elinor's interminable housewifery lessons. One morning she made me memorize the herbs most commonly used to keep away fleas, moths, and other household vermin, until I thought I should scream. I think the frustration may have been mutual, because my aunt suddenly announced that she felt one of her headaches coming on. She said this was my fault for trying her patience, and she bade me to walk in the garden and leave her in peace until it was time for the midday meal.

But by this time I was fuming with boredom and

misery, and in my turbulent mood, the garden seemed no less confining than the house. At my aunt's insistence, the shrubs and walkways were kept as trim and orderly as her own embroidery. I paced restlessly between the flower beds, feeling as helpless as any prisoner in the Tower of London. *No wonder poets refuse to give their heroines happy endings*, I thought miserably. *It is because girls' lives are so narrow in real life.*

It was nearing the end of February and we were having a few days of false spring. In the shelter of the walled garden, the sunlight was unexpectedly warm and signs of new growth were everywhere. But I scarcely registered the tiny buds or the vivid spikes of crocus. What was the use of beauty if my days were to be spent indoors fussing over stains? What was the use of hopes and dreams if you were only a girl?

Meg came out and emptied a bucket of dirty water down the sinkhole. When she saw me, she gave a little jump of surprise. "Miss! I did not see you there!" Her expression changed. "Why, what ails you, miss? You look so sad."

"I was just thinking," I sighed. "My life will change

a great deal when Sabine leaves home."

Meg's eyes were sympathetic. "You will miss your sister, I am sure."

"Not just that. I will have to give up all hope of adventures—and all hope of ever going to the play-house," I added gloomily. On our walks together, Meg often entertained me with colorful descriptions of her experiences at the playhouse.

She looked thoughtful. "'Tis a pity, for my brother Kit told me I can visit him at the Rose any time I like."

I gasped. "Meg, I've had a wonderful idea! It is Cook's afternoon off. Why don't you slip away and we'll go to the Rose together?"

"I can't, miss," she said regretfully. "I have work to do."

But I refused to take no for an answer. I was desperate to have even the smallest taste of freedom. This adventure would be my first and might well be my last.

"No one will know," I assured her. "My father is away on business. And my aunt and Sabine have an appointment at the dressmaker's, so they'll be gone for hours."

"I don't know, miss," she said doubtfully.

"Oh, say you will, please?" I pleaded. "It'll be easy, you'll see! We'll get a ferry across to Southwark, see the play, say hello to Kit, and be back before anyone knows we've gone."

Then I groaned with frustration. "Alas, I have no money for the ferry. I suppose we could walk across London Bridge. But I cannot bear the sight of those pitiful heads." I suppressed a shudder. Men and women judged guilty of certain crimes were beheaded, and their gory heads were placed on spikes at London Bridge, and also at Temple Bar, as a dreadful warning to others.

"Those criminals do not deserve your pity," said Meg severely. "In life they were but villains, fit only to feed the crows. All manner of scoundrels live down our way, and they care for no one but themselves, miss."

I pictured the screaming birds swooping down to peck at those terrible, sightless eyes. "Perhaps if I ran very fast," I said bravely.

Meg went into peals of laughter. "You need not

cross the bridge at all, miss! My Uncle Alfred is a waterman. We'll borrow one of his boats and row ourselves across."

I threw my arms around her and caught the scent of the rosemary flowers Meg used to rinse her hair. "That means you'll do it! Oh, thank you, Meg!"

She pushed me away, still laughing. "Miss," she protested, "embraces are for your relatives and sweet-hearts, not for such as me."

"Embraces are for friends, too," I said.

Meg pretended she hadn't heard. "I will watch for you by the gate, miss, once Mistress Elinor and Miss Sabine have gone out."

After Meg had finished her tasks, we crept out of the house and ran down to the jetty.

"My uncle will not miss this one," Meg said.

I peered into the shabby little boat. "There's water in the bottom."

Meg clambered in, making it rock. "Boats always leak," she said carelessly. "We'll just bail it out with this." She waved a pail.

I felt nervous as Meg rowed us out into the river, but

we reached the opposite shore so swiftly that I began to wonder why I did not cross over the water to South-wark every day! Meg tied the boat to a post, and we made our way toward the playhouse under the spire of Saint Mary of the Ferry.

Bawdy singing floated from the taverns. Dilapidated houses were crowded together so closely that it was impossible to see where one ended and its neighbor began. Women in torn, gaudy finery shrieked to each other across the stinking alleys, sounding as fierce and raucous as seagulls.

I felt as if I had strayed into a foreign country. London's south bank felt thrilling and distinctly dangerous. On my side of the Thames, no one paid me any attention, but here ragged children pointed and called out rude comments about my fine clothes. Two women nudged each other as we passed, and one said, "Oh, ain't she a sweet little rosebud!" They both burst out laughing, showing blackened teeth. I felt a flicker of fear and found myself holding my breath until we were safely past.

A drunken man staggered up to me. "Allow me to

offer you my protection, little mistress," he slurred, and he went to take my arm.

Meg gave him a violent poke in the chest. "Lay one finger on my mistress, you fat lummox, and I'll make you wish you'd never been born," she blazed. Mumbling his apologies, the man stumbled away.

"You must not stare around you so, miss," Meg told me in a low voice. "Fix your eyes straight ahead; then no one will trouble you."

At last we came in sight of the Rose Theatre, with its flag fluttering above a great thatched roof. Strong, clear voices boomed from inside the walls. *We are too late!* I thought in dismay. *The play must have started already.*

Meg marched up to one of the men outside and murmured in his ear. He grinned and opened the door a crack, and we slipped through. But nothing had prepared me for the sight of so many human beings gathered in one place, and I almost turned and ran. Meg firmly yanked me inside, and the door closed behind us.

I took a faltering step, vaguely aware of hazelnut

shells scrunching beneath my feet. Astonishment made me speechless for once. The playhouse was so big and grand!

Beautifully carved wooden galleries rose in tiers on either side of me. Better-off playgoers sat here. They were able to pay a few pence extra to sit in the dry, with a good view of the stage. I couldn't help glancing curiously at the upper balcony. I'd overheard my aunt say that this was where shameless women displayed their charms for men to see. I had a blurred impression of garishly painted faces and pale bosoms half-exposed above low-cut bodices, but I can't say I found these women any more shocking than many I had seen in the street.

Immediately in front of me was the open yard where the poorer members of the audience, known as the groundlings, stood in all weathers to watch the performance. Hundreds of Londoners had come to see the play: butchers in dirty aprons, porters, tailors, fishwives, poor scholars, and little apprentice boys, all milling about, chatting to friends, or buying hazelnuts or apples from the food sellers.

But it was not only the scale of the playhouse that took my breath away. It was also its beauty. The Rose was so skillfully decorated that I could almost believe I stood in a fine palace, looking at real marble pillars decorated with gold leaf, not crudely painted wood. To think this wonderful place was just across the river and I had not seen it until now!

Meg smiled to see my face. "Pretty, isn't it, miss?" she asked happily. "There are so many colors, like a peacock's tail!"

Unfortunately, the stink of so many people packed closely together was making me feel faint. *I wish I had brought my pomander,* I thought queasily.

Meg saw me changing color and swiftly produced an orange from somewhere in her skirts. "Rub the peel on your wrists, miss," she grinned. "The scent will mask this bad stench." Her remedy worked, and I immediately felt better.

"We must get close to the stage," she advised me, "or we will see nothing but these fellows' dirty doublets." She towed me through the crowd. I clung to Meg's hand, terrified of losing her in the crush.

I couldn't see where we were going. I could only hear the actors' voices ringing over my head.

Then my skin broke into gooseflesh as I saw the stage at last!

It was more magical than I had ever dreamed, with its gorgeous blue-painted heavens and glittering suns, stars, and moons. But most magical of all were the actors themselves, striding about in their brightly colored costumes. I was so excited that I thought my heart would burst.

"Will you ask someone what play this is?" I asked Meg.

She spoke to a young man beside her. "He says 'tis by some new playwright—Will Shakespeare, he thinks his name is."

"Oh, yes! Master Hart thinks highly of him," I said excitedly.

Then a stirring drumbeat filled the air, and nothing else mattered except the play.

Once a pigeon flew in through the great open roof with a whirl of wings, making me look up. And I was astonished to see cloudy London skies over my head.

I had completely forgotten where I was, just as I had forgotten that the person playing the wicked heroine was really a boy! Women were not allowed to act on the stage, but the actor in his wig and gown played the part so convincingly that I was swiftly persuaded that he was genuinely female. I was so caught up in the play that when the heroine pretended she didn't know the humble shepherd who was her father, I booed and hissed angrily along with everybody else.

When the play was over, Meg took me backstage to the tiring house, where the actors changed costumes and rested between scenes. It was so busy that no one noticed us come in. Two young actors were having a pretend sword fight. I noticed that their costumes seemed shabbier and dirtier than they had up on the stage.

I recognized Kit at once. He had exactly the same warm smile as Meg, though he was taller and sturdier. He was sitting on an upturned barrel, sewing gold braid onto one of the costumes and trading good-humored insults with the actor who had played the shepherd. Kit's face lit up when he saw his sister.

"Why, Meg, what did you think of the play?"

Meg introduced me to her brother and he proudly took us to see the theatre's properties, the objects that the actors used to make the plays seem true to life: suits of armor, a royal throne, a witch's cauldron, a golden fleece, and a terrifyingly evil snake.

Kit pointed out a trapdoor cleverly concealed behind the painted heavens. "We produce many theatrical effects up there," he explained. "There is an iron ball we roll around to make thunder, and ropes and pulleys that make a man appear to fly through the air. To the groundlings it looks as if 'tis done by magic, but it takes three of us stagehands to keep him air-borne!" He laughed. "Four if 'tis Ned Scrivener."

There was a theatrical "hell" in the cellar, too, with a smoke machine and another hidden trapdoor so that ghosts and devils could burst up dramatically through the stage.

At last Meg said regretfully, "We must go, before they miss me at the house."

"Can't we go onto the stage for just a moment?" I pleaded.

"All right, miss," she sighed. "But we must not stay long."

We tiptoed onto the stage of the playhouse, and the soles of my feet began to tingle as if some invisible magic still lingered from the play.

I was filled with yearning. If only girls were permitted to act upon the stage. Then I could join the theatre like Kit. And when summer came and London's theatres closed, I would wander the countryside with my fellow players, thrilling audiences with my performances. Perhaps I would even write plays like Master Shakespeare's.

Meg was anxiously trying to get my attention. She tugged at my sleeve. "Miss, 'tis getting dark."

I was horrified to see that the sun had almost set. "Meg, you should have told me!"

"I've been trying, miss," she wailed. "But it's like you were in a trance. Oh, miss, we must run, or I'll be in terrible trouble."

We picked up our skirts and ran all the way to the boat. Meg began to row frantically across the darkening river. The evening was unusually mild for the time of year. Suddenly we heard music drifting through the air. A barge floated past, lit by flaming torches. It was long and low, and its carved prow gleamed with gold leaf. Inside was a gauzy canopy decorated with twinkling moons and stars. Through this shimmering veil I saw lords and ladies wearing strange golden masks. One lord softly played a lute.

The sight was so dreamlike that I felt as if I were in a play myself. *I'm having a real adventure at last!* I thought. But as I gazed enchanted, I felt water sloshing around my feet.

"Meg, the boat is filling up with water!" I started bailing wildly with the pail, but the water was coming in too quickly. Soon it had risen past my ankles.

Meg dropped her oars and began scooping out water in her cupped hands. "Bail faster, or we shall both be drowned!" she sobbed.

"Please help us!" I screamed to the people in the barge, but they were too far away in a glittering world of their own and did not hear.

Just as I was convinced we would go under the water forever, I heard a steady splash of oars. A light came bobbing toward us. I caught the reek of burning pitch from a torch, and a rough voice came booming across the water. Meg's uncle had come to save us.

Without a word, he helped us out of the sinking boat and rowed us to shore. He hurried us through the dark, silent streets to my father's house. I kept waiting for Meg's uncle to scold us for sinking his boat. But when he saw that we were safely home, he just bid us a gruff good night and strode off into the darkness.

I was in such a panic that I ran into the house without another word to Meg. *I must change my clothes before anyone sees me,* I thought. To my dismay, my pretty slippers were ruined. I took them off and went squelching upstairs in my wet stockings. But before I could reach my chamber, an angry voice made me freeze.

"Isabel Campion, where have you been?" my aunt demanded.

5 Banished!

I was alone in the schoolroom. Weak spring sunshine filtered through the tiny panes of glass, warming my back as I sat working at my embroidery. I had been here every day since my aunt had caught me sneaking upstairs in my wet things: seven long, lonely, frightening days.

My aunt said that my behavior was so shocking that she could not possibly punish me herself, but must wait for my father's return. "Until then you are forbidden to leave the house," she commanded.

"May I read my books, aunt?" I asked anxiously.

"No, you may not read your books!" My aunt's voice had sounded like a whip. "Your head is filled with enough foolish moonshine as it is. You will use this period of solitude to improve your needlework and reflect upon your appalling behavior."

I bent my head over my sampler. I was stitching a row of tiny primroses with delicate yellow silk. Sounds floated up from below: rumbling cart wheels from the street, the clatter of pans in the kitchen, Joan's sudden bark of laughter, and the rhythmic *swish-swoosh* as Meg scrubbed the flagstones in the hall. The world was going on around me just as if nothing had happened.

My aunt swept in and inspected my embroidery with a scornful expression. "Tsk, tsk! There are more loops behind than a patch of bindweed. Unpick it and start again." And she swept out with a rustle of skirts.

I began to unpick my sunny little stitches one by one. Both my aunt and I knew there was nothing wrong with my work. I had been doing embroidery since I was four years old. But I also knew that I deserved to be punished, for my crimes were even worse than Aunt Elinor imagined. My aunt knew only that I had mysteriously fallen in the water and ruined my clothes. I would not tell her more for fear of adding to my offense.

She did not know I had helped to steal a boat, then sank it in the Thames on the way back from a play-house. And she had no idea Meg had been with me. Meg and I had been careful to avoid each other since that night.

It seems that God did not intend girls to be brave and bold like their brothers, I thought miserably. *If they try, people just get hurt.*

I heard halting footsteps and looked up. It was Alice, with some warm gingerbread for me. "You have had a long week, my honey," she said sympathetically, "shut indoors with your needle and thread."

"I fear my aunt would like to unpick me like this embroidery and start again," I said forlornly. "Every-thing I do displeases her."

Alice shook her head. "Your aunt cares for you more

than you know. When we discovered you were missing, she was beside herself. Grown men fear to walk London's streets alone after dark, and you are but a little maid of twelve summers."

"Oh, we weren't alone! Meg's uncle brought us home." My voice faltered as I realized what I'd said.

"I know all about it," Alice said quietly. "I had to lend the poor child some of my clothes until hers could be dried."

It had not occurred to me that Meg owned only the shabby little dress she stood up in. My face burned as I remembered how I had just run off, leaving her in her wet things.

"She could have lost her job because of you," Alice went on. "And her family depends on her wages."

I swallowed hard. "Thank you for not telling my aunt," I said humbly.

"I did not do it for you alone, child, but for your lady mother's sake. How her heart would ache if she could see you now."

I threw myself into her arms. "Please don't say that," I wailed. "I feel as if I have been holding my breath all week. I'm scared, Alice. What will my father do to me?"

Alice stroked my cheek. "He's a good man. He will do what he thinks is best."

"I don't see why life must be so terrible," I wept.

"Aye, it is terrible, my honey, and also wonderful and all things between," Alice said comfortingly. "Do not always want what you cannot have, for such discontent blinds you to your own good fortune. You are in good health. You live in a fine big house, with a father who cares for you. Sometimes we do not appreciate what we have till it's gone."

She gave me a sad smile. With a pang of shame I remembered that all Alice's family had died in the plague many years ago, leaving her alone in the world. "I will try to do better," I promised her.

Much later I crept down the hall and waited by the kitchen door. Meg hurried out at last, looking flustered. When she saw me, she jumped with fright. I put my finger to my lips and slipped the parcel of gingerbread into Meg's pocket.

To my astonishment she burst into tears. "Oh, miss! I should never have taken you in that boat."

I quickly put my hand over her mouth. "Sssh, someone will hear!"

"'Tis true!" Her voice cracked with distress. "I was just showing off, my uncle says. Oh, miss, how can you ever forgive me—I almost drowned you!"

"No, no, it's me who should be sorry," I whispered. "I said I was your friend, but I thought only of myself. I hope you will forgive me."

By this time I was crying, too.

On the other side of the door, Joan burst loudly into song.

Meg and I exchanged incredulous glances. "She sounds just like a donkey braying," I whispered.

We both giggled through our tears.

Meg wiped her eyes. "Look at us. We are a fine pair."

I caught at her hand. "It was beautiful, wasn't it, when that barge floated past?" I said softly.

I saw Meg's eyes sparkle in the dim light of the hallway. "Aye, beautiful, miss. Though I did fear it might be the last sight I saw in this world!"

Night had fallen by the time my father returned. I was watching at the window and saw a lighted torch bobbing through the dark. I heard the chink of coins and my father's deep voice thanking the linkboy for lighting him home.

Normally I would run to meet him, and he'd give me a great bear hug and say, "Have you missed your father, kitten?" Then I'd keep him company while he ate his meal, and later he'd give me some little trinket he had bought for me on his travels.

But tonight I waited until I was called. I waited for what seemed hours with only a flickering stump of candle for company. I felt strangely breathless, as if I'd been running too fast. At last I heard someone coming upstairs.

Sabine's voice said, "Isabel?"

I jumped up and took my candle to the door.

"Our father wants to see you." My sister's voice was tight with unhappiness.

"Is he very disappointed with me?" I asked fearfully.

"We are all disappointed, Isabel, for you have ruined everything."

To my dismay, Sabine burst into tears and fled across the landing.

I made my way downstairs, feeling sick with apprehension. I knew I was no longer my father's precious child, his funny chatterbox, his mischievous kitten. I was a great tall girl, a foolish young female, and I had failed to know my place.

I knocked at the door of my father's writing closet and went in.

"You sent for me, sir?"

My father sat at his desk, writing in his smooth, flowing script.

Aunt Elinor stood at his side, nervously clasping and unclasping her hands.

My father looked up. "I have been told of your misbehavior, Isabel." He sounded so cold that I felt more frightened than if he had raged at me.

"I am very sorry for offending you, sir," I said humbly.

"That is not good enough," he said in the same cold tone. "You owe me an explanation, Isabel. You know full well that you are not allowed to roam around after dark. What were you doing out alone at that time of night, to come home in that bedraggled condition?"

"I am afraid I cannot tell you, sir." I heard my voice quiver. I hated concealing the truth from my father, but if I told him what had really happened, Meg would lose her job, and all her family would suffer.

He gave me an incredulous look. "And that is all you have to say?"

My knees had started to shake. I feared they would refuse to hold me up, but somehow I managed to stay standing. "That is all I have to say, sir," I said bravely.

My father jumped to his feet, and for a moment I feared he might actually strike me. "I can scarcely believe you are your mother's daughter," he thundered. "It is bad enough that you betrayed my trust and disobeyed me. Now you show complete disrespect for me, and I will not tolerate that, do you understand?"

The cruel words had cut me to the quick, but I just said in a low voice, "I give you my word that it will never happen again."

My father's voice was cold and contemptuous. "You are right, Isabel. It will *not* happen again. Your aunt and I have agreed that things cannot go on as they are."

And he sat down again and began rereading the letter on his desk.

My father seemed to have changed into a terrifying stranger. I felt as if I no longer knew this man who spoke to me so harshly. He was staring at me as if he did not know me, either. I couldn't bear it. This had all come about because I had stupidly insisted on having an adventure. Now I had to choose between hurting one or the other of the two people I loved best, and I couldn't bear it. I felt utterly helpless. There seemed to be nothing I could do or say to make things right between us.

"I am so sorry," I whispered. But I knew it was too late for apologies.

My father drew a deep breath. "You will remember that your mother had a half-sister, your Aunt de Vere?"

I twisted my hands in my kirtle to stop them trembling. "Yes, sir. She was at my mother's funeral."

"Your Aunt de Vere is a widow. Like many widows she is very religious and has devoted herself to serving others. She has asked several times if I would send you to stay with her. I didn't approve of this convention of sending children away to live with strangers, so I always refused."

I nodded again, for by this time I was far too frightened to speak.

"In light of the recent circumstances, I have changed my mind. I have written to your aunt accepting her offer. If she is still agreeable, you will go to live with her in Northamptonshire as soon as it can be arranged."

I found my voice. "But sir, I—"

"Silence, Isabel!" he thundered. "You have grown too wild of late. Your wings must be clipped. You will live with your aunt in the country and continue your education until such a time—" my father's voice broke suddenly. "Until I decide to send for you."

He signed his letter, and without looking up he said, "This means, of course, that you will not be attending your sister's wedding. This has distressed her greatly. But you left me no choice."

I felt as if I were trapped in a nightmare. Surely, my father could not just send me away! This was my home, my family. I could scarcely remember this mysterious aunt. I had endured my mother's funeral wrapped in a private fog of misery, and I retained only a vague impression of a tall, large-boned woman with uncomfortably piercing blue eyes.

My father carefully folded the parchment, sealed it with wax, and set his mark upon it with his signet ring. "The letter will be sent tomorrow, Isabel," he said huskily. "You may go."

Numb with shock, I went up to my chamber.

I could hear Sabine's muffled sobs coming from under the bedcovers. I wanted to put my arms around her and say how sorry I was for making her so unhappy, but I didn't dare.

A frightened wail came from across the landing, but Sabine continued to weep and Alice was downstairs, so I went in to my little sister.

"There, there, little one, 'twas just a dream. I'm here now," I whispered. They were the same words my nurse used to comfort me when I was a little girl, in the days when my father was still proud of me. I perched on my baby sister's small, narrow bed and took her in my arms. I felt her soft hair tickle my cheek and smelled the pungent herbal salve Alice had smeared on her chest to help her breathe more easily.

"Don't cry, little sweeting. I'll sing you a lullaby. Would you like that?"

Hope nodded solemnly, her fat tears still rolling down her cheeks, and I sat softly singing lullabies to my little sister until the two of us fell asleep.

6 Brigands on the Road

Raindrops splattered my new traveling cloak.

Everything had been bought new for my journey—boots, gloves, even my travel bags were new. All these unfamiliar things made me feel as if I were playing a part. This wasn't really happening. It wasn't Isabel Campion who was being sent away. It was a girl in a play.

"Think you can get up by yourself, little mistress?"

I could tell that Aunt de Vere's servant disapproved of the spoiled girl he was forced to accompany on the long journey from London to Northamptonshire. And he clearly expected a Londoner to sit in the saddle like a sack of potatoes.

"I can manage, thank you, John," I said stiffly. "I have ridden many times." I swung myself up into the

saddle, and John nimbly sprang up in front of me.
All kinds of alarming characters haunted England's
public highways, from mumbling Tom o'Bedlams to
dangerous highwaymen and brigands. Even fine lords
and ladies thought it prudent to ride pillion with a
trusted manservant.

My family had come outside to watch me leave.
They waited in front of the house, as silent and somber
as figures in a painting. Alice stood on the step with
my baby sister in her arms. Alice whispered something
to Hope, and my sister waved dutifully, but her eyes
were puzzled.

My father had managed to avoid looking at me
these past weeks. Now suddenly he fixed his eyes on
mine as if he feared he would never see me again.

I felt a surge of joy. *It isn't too late!* I thought wildly.
It was just a test. Now he'll tell me I can stay. Perhaps
if I'd begged him for his forgiveness then, my father
would have changed his mind. But I was too hurt to
beg, and he was too proud, so I just looked down and
pretended to fiddle with the fastening of my glove,
and the moment passed. I lifted my chin. "Ride on

when you are ready, John."

John made a clicking sound. The horse tossed its
mane and trotted off over the gleaming wet cobbles,
its harness jingling.

"Miss, wait!" Meg came flying around the back of
the house, her shawl over her head. She ran up and
pressed something into my palm. "'Tis a charm to keep
you safe on your journey. My mother threaded ribbon
through it so that you can wear it around your neck."
I looked down at the round dark stone with a second
glistening rose-colored stone embedded in its center,
like a heart. Meg closed my gloved fingers over her
lucky charm. "Be brave, miss," she said tearfully.
"And if God wills, we shall meet again."

"Thank you, Meg," I said softly. "I shall keep this
always."

"We must go, little mistress," said John in his
disapproving voice. "We have many miles to travel.
We must go the long way round to deliver a parcel of
your aunt's good physic to an apothecary near London
Bridge."

I didn't look back as we rode away from my father's

house. I sat proudly in the saddle, telling myself I would not cry. Since I had to leave my home and family, I would have preferred to go galloping out of the city at once, putting them behind me as swiftly as possible. But instead we had to make our way along the narrow, crowded streets to the other side of London. The horse was unused to city traffic, and John had to coax the nervous beast between shouting street vendors, dirty farm carts, and fine coaches. At last we reached the premises of a well-respected London apothecary. I had to wait on a drafty bench while the elderly apothecary scrutinized a letter from my Aunt de Vere through a magnifying glass, then wrote her a lengthy reply. I felt strangely unreal, as if I were no longer a person, just another parcel that my aunt's servant had to deliver.

But eventually we joined the stream of riders, carts, and pedestrians flowing over London Bridge. The bridge was really just a continuation of the narrow, cobbled street, with houses and shops jostling closely on either side. At the far end of the bridge, a mob of screaming crows pecked at the grisly heads on their poles. But today I passed them in a daze of misery.

Only one thought came again and again like the beat of a drum. *He sent me away, he sent me away, he sent me away.*

We gradually left the noise and stink of the city behind. After Islington, the houses became more widely spaced until there were only dripping trees and hedgerows on either side of the queen's highway.

Several hours into our journey, our horse stumbled, and we were lucky not to be thrown off. We dismounted and found that he had cast a shoe. We walked the horse to the nearest village, some miles away, and waited in the local inn while the blacksmith fitted new horseshoes.

This delay meant we could not put up at the post house in Saint Albans, as Aunt de Vere had arranged. Instead we were forced to stay at a tumbledown village tavern, where the innkeeper was obviously drunk. Our journey to Northamptonshire should have taken us only two days. Now we'd have to spend a second night on the road.

The innkeeper's slatternly wife fetched us food, but the sight of the greasy stew nauseated me. I was almost falling asleep in my chair, and I asked if I might go to bed. But the woman explained that I must wait until she finished her work. As a young girl traveling without a female chaperone, it was not thought proper for me to sleep alone, and so I was forced to share a bed with the innkeeper's wife while her husband slept downstairs.

This arrangement was highly unpleasant. I don't think the woman had ever cut her toenails in her life, and she snored so loudly that the bed rattled against the floorboards. I am sure there were fleas in the bed, too, for when I put on my gown the next day I found angry red bites all over me.

When I came downstairs, the innkeeper's wife presented me with a slab of cold, evil-smelling pie. "Thank you. I will eat it on the road," I said politely, privately planning to dispose of it in a convenient hedge.

I ducked through the tavern door, feeling lightheaded with exhaustion, and found Aunt de Vere's servant in the courtyard, saddling the horse.

The rain had stopped, and spring sunlight glinted

off the puddles in the lanes as we resumed our journey. John told me that if all went well, we would reach my aunt's by noon next day.

Small birds sang all around us, and every bush was crowded with tiny buds. Violets and primroses scented the air, and, for the first time, I felt relieved to be out of the stink of London. After some hours, we left the main highway and entered an ancient forest.

"I hope you are not afraid, little mistress, among so many trees," said John grudgingly. "But 'twill shorten our journey by several hours."

I felt faintly uneasy, but after my sleepless night, the rhythmic rise and fall of our horse made me drowsy, and I fell into a light doze.

I awoke to furious shouts as several masked men on horseback came charging out of nowhere.

John swore and dug his heels into the horse's flanks. The first brigand drew level and made a lunge at the reins as the others closed in around us. Our horse reared in terror. By some miracle I clung on, but John fell heavily, striking his head on a tree root.

I sprang down, screaming and beating at the nearest

man with my fists. He shook me off. "Scream away, my little maid," he said calmly. "For there's no one to hear."

He turned John's limp body over with his foot, and I saw dark blood staining the servant's face and throat. "Dead," the man said with satisfaction. He sprang onto our horse and the brigands galloped away, taking my possessions and leaving me alone in the forest.

7 A Voice in the Dark

"Help! Murder! Won't anybody help me?"

I called and pleaded until I was hoarse, but there was no reply except the sound of my own voice echoing eerily back from the trees. It was just as the brigand had said. There was no one to hear my cries.

I had never been alone in the woods before, and every rustling leaf and snapping twig made me freeze, for fear of what lurked invisibly behind the trees. The light was fading fast, and with a sinking heart I realized I would never find my way out of the forest by nightfall.

I was beginning to despair, when I suddenly thought of Nicolette, the bold slave girl in Master Hart's tale. *What would Nicolette do in my place?* I wondered. I decided she would sensibly climb a tree while there was still enough daylight to see by, and so should I.

I'd be safe from wild beasts until morning came and I could continue on my journey.

I chose a stout oak with good footholds and hoisted myself into its branches. For an anxious moment I hung suspended, too scared to go on, yet unable to get back down. Eventually I found the courage to climb higher, until I reached a reasonably secure resting place. Then I wedged myself against the trunk and prepared to settle for the night.

After a while my mind began to play strange tricks. I imagined that I could smell wood smoke, and I thought I could see firelight flickering in the dusk.

I saw a man die today, I thought tremulously. *It's no wonder I am seeing things that are not there.*

Soon I began to hear things, too. I heard a tuneful male voice singing Meg's favorite song, "Bonny Sweet Robin Is All My Joy."

All the tiny hairs rose up on my neck, and my breathing quickened. Was some malicious spirit trying to frighten me out of my wits?

Suddenly the singer cursed. "A pox upon Ned Scrivener! I told him that we were out of salt, yet he paid me no heed."

That is no ghost! I thought. And I scrambled down from my perch so eagerly that I skinned my hands on the way down.

Using the firelight to guide me, I groped my way among the trees, colliding with stumps and tripping over fallen branches, until I arrived at a sort of gypsy camp. A battered old stewpot bubbled over a fire. Delicious smells of onions and gravy leaked from under the lid, making my belly growl with hunger.

Nearby stood a painted tilt-cart crammed with baskets and bundles. A boy was ransacking one of the bundles, muttering, "No salt in here, alas. Stew without salt! That won't improve Master Pink's temper. Ah, well. I will add a dash of strong ale, and perchance he will not notice."

He turned back to the pot, and I saw his face by the light of the flames. I was so startled that I cried, "Kit! Is it you?"

Meg's brother started with surprise, and his hand flew to the little knife at his belt. He stared around wildly. "Whoever speaks, let him take care, for

I am armed and dangerous!" he shouted.

I stepped from the shadows, and he gasped in amazement.

"I know you. You are Meg's little mistress that she almost drowned in the Thames!"

Relief and hunger made me dizzy. I swayed on my feet. Kit exclaimed in concern and caught me just before I fell. He half-carried me into the firelight and quickly made me comfortable on a pile of sacks. Then he ladled out some of the stew onto a wooden platter and commanded me to eat.

I ate it all greedily, wiping my platter clean with a crust of bread. "Oh, Kit, thank you!" I said earnestly. "I have never been so hungry in my life!"

Kit had been sitting quietly, but I could see he was struggling to contain his curiosity. "But how did you come to be wandering alone in the forest, little mistress?" His face grew awed as I told him how my aunt's servant had been killed. He pointed to Meg's lucky stone hanging around my neck. "My sister's charm protected you, little mistress! Those ruffians could have kidnapped you, or worse. But you are safe now. You can spend the night in the forest with us."

"Who is 'us'?" I asked uncertainly. "And what are *you* doing out here in the forest, Kit?"

Meg's brother laughed. "Never fear, mistress. I have not joined the outlaws! I am traveling with some other actors from the Rose. I have now been apprenticed to Master Pink. That means I can play minor parts, as well as being general dogsbody. The others walked into town to advertise our play tomorrow, leaving me to make supper."

"You are actually traveling with the players?" I breathed. A shiver went through me, and I experienced the same magical feeling I had felt when I set foot on the stage at the playhouse.

Kit was busily dishing me up a second helping of stew. He suddenly caught sight of my face. "Why, miss, you look as if you have seen a ghost!"

But I couldn't bring myself to explain to Kit how I had stood on the stage at the Rose and dreamed of wandering the countryside with traveling players. A few hours earlier, Aunt de Vere's servant had been brutally killed. And when I failed to appear at my aunt's, my family would assume I was dead, too. It didn't feel right for my selfish dream to come true under such desperate circumstances.

Kit was watching me sympathetically. "Why were you traveling through the forest in the first place?" he prompted me.

My face burned with shame. "I was on my way to live with my aunt in Northamptonshire. My father was displeased with my behavior, so he sent me away to learn to be a fine lady." Tears welled in my eyes as the gravity of my situation sank in. "Oh, Kit, when I don't arrive at Aunt de Vere's, my family will think I am dead. I must find someone to take me to her estate in Northamptonshire. Can you help me?"

Kit fell silent, and for some moments he stared into the fire. I sensed that he was struggling to find the right words. At last he cleared his throat.

"Meg thinks the world of you, little mistress," he said gravely. "I would not feel easy in my mind if I were to entrust you to the care of strangers. I would gladly take you to your aunt myself, but I doubt that Master Pink could spare me, for we are but a small company. But in three weeks we are to perform in the town of Northampton, on our way to Stourbridge Fair. Would you consider staying with us until then, and then I can deliver you safely to your aunt's?"

"You do not mean it!" I gasped. "Oh, Kit, that is a wonderful idea!"

Meg's brother shook his head. "There is more," he said awkwardly. "I mean no disrespect, little mistress, but you would have to disguise yourself in boys' clothing. If the other players were to suspect that you were a girl, they would refuse to let you travel with us."

I felt a thrill of excitement! "I don't mind disguising myself! I'll do it gladly!"

"Be not so hasty, mistress," said Kit. "Our life is arduous. Some days we earn so little, we can hardly feed ourselves. Yesterday, some scurvy fellow stole Master Pink's beaver hat with all our takings, so we can't afford to put up at the tavern but must camp in the woods like Robin Hood and his merry men."

But I thought Kit's plan sounded perfect. I hated to cause my family any more distress, but I had little choice. If we met up with some travelers making for

Northamptonshire more directly, I could always send word to my aunt. And no matter what Kit said, I was convinced that traveling with the players was going to be a wonderful adventure!

"You had bad luck," I told him earnestly. "That's all. If I join you, your luck may change."

Kit hesitated. "Mistress, do you honestly think you can convince them that you are a boy, day in and day out, for three whole weeks?"

"I know I can," I said confidently. "Now lend me your knife. I am going to cut off my hair."

Kit and I agreed that I would pretend to be my brother, Robert. We would tell everyone that brigands had robbed me, taking not only my horse and money but the very clothes I stood up in. Kit found me an old doublet, a shirt, hose, and a worn velvet cap, then tactfully turned his back while I put them on.

"Boys can get dressed so quickly!" I marveled. "And their clothes are much more comfortable!" When Kit turned around, I swept off my cap and bowed as I had seen my male relatives do. "How do I look, sir?"

"Very fine, Master Robert," he grinned. "Except for

your hair, which looks as if a mad dog had chewed it. I had better neaten the ends."

I started toward him, but he wagged his finger. "Your walk needs more swagger, Master Robert! Real boys do not skip and prance."

When the other players returned, they were not the exuberant crowd of actors I had pictured but half a dozen weary-looking men, leading a thin, shabby-looking donkey. The actors' clothes were worn and threadbare. But I saw that each man had added some brave theatrical flourish—a peacock's feather in his cap, a festoon of ribbons upon his sleeves, or tarnished gold rosettes upon his muddy shoes.

The tallest and most handsome of the players had a vivid pink silk rose pinned to his doublet. His wild black hair was dramatically streaked with white, and his dark eyes glittered. I thought he looked exactly like a gypsy king.

"That is Master Jasper Pink," Kit hissed to me. "You had better bow to him."

I scrambled to my feet and made a deep bow.

"And who is this strange little sprite?" Master Pink

asked in a disparaging tone. He had an actor's voice, rich and warmly resonant.

Kit told him our story, adding that I had assured them of a large reward when I was returned to my wealthy aunt. "Master Robert says he can make himself useful," he said eagerly. "He reads wondrous well, so he can prompt us in our parts, and he can sing, dance, and play the lute."

Master Pink looked suspicious. "You have gotten to know him remarkably well in such a short time."

"Oh, that is my fault," I said quickly. "My father says I should have been a girl! He says I babble any foolishness that comes into my head."

I waited, with my heart pounding, to see if Master Pink was convinced by my first speech as Robert Campion.

He looked me over frowningly. "There will be a reward, you say?"

"My aunt will wish to thank you handsomely," I said earnestly.

"Hmm." Master Pink paced in glowering silence until the tension became unbearable. Then he broke into a dazzling showman's smile. "We welcome you to our company of players, little brother!"

A hideous trumpeting made everyone burst into laughter. Master Pink patted the donkey affectionately. "And so says Mistress Delilah!"

8 An Actor Born

Boom-boom, boom-boom, boom-boom.

The beating of Ned Scrivener's drum filled my head as we capered through the streets of the little market town. I'd been traveling with the players for nearly a week and the routine was rapidly becoming second nature to me. I had big blisters on my heels and my belly was gurgling with hunger, but I was a player now, so like Sam Tilly and Toby Fettle, I clowned and cart-wheeled as if I had springs in my shoes.

Kit accompanied Ned's drum on a little pipe, occasionally showering passersby with dried rose petals, though not many, for our supplies were getting low. Master Pink was too dignified to perform tumbling tricks. He strode around, swirling his cloak with its dramatic scarlet lining, aiming smoldering smiles at the wives and daughters, and urging them to come to the Angel to see our play.

By the time we reached the market square, we had gathered an admiring flock of followers. Master Pink muttered, "One, two, three!" This was my cue to begin singing the round known as "My Poor Bird." The other players joined in, one after another, until our voices sounded exactly like wonderful peals of bells, and the crowd applauded and cried out for more.

But our intention was only to whet their appetites, and I sang out saucily, "If our song pleases you, come to the Angel at two of the clock and we will enchant you and drive away dull cares!"

Having advertised our presence to the townsfolk, we all made our way back to the Angel Inn and began to get ready for the next performance. Kit and I made sure the properties were in good order, while Ned and the others laid boards across the back of Delilah's cart to form a stage.

The innkeeper's daughter came out with bread and ale for our midday meal. Her little brother toddled out after her. He tripped and fell sprawling on the cobbles. Without thinking, I picked him up to comfort him.

"You'll make someone a good wife one day, Brother Robert," Ned teased.

"Did you never comfort your little brothers and sisters when they were injured, Master Scrivener?" I retorted quickly.

Sam pretended to be horrified. "Let us pray not. One look at Ned's ugly mug is surely injury enough!"

I set the little boy gently back on his feet. I had not realized it would be such a strain, having to remember to act like a boy day in, day out. So far I had covered any slips. Now all my work had been nearly undone by the touch of that soft baby cheek, which had reminded me painfully of Hope.

What if Joan was right? I thought. *What if the angels*

come to carry my little sister away while I am roaming the countryside putting on plays in taverns? What if I never see her again in this world?

Master Pink was hungrily helping himself to the landlord's food. "Come, fill your belly, lad!" he called. "This may be your last chance until Banbury!"

I mumbled that I must first catch up Philomena's hem where Toby had torn it dancing the pavane in the wedding scene, and I used my sewing as a ploy to hide the tears that had unexpectedly filled my eyes.

A few days later, disaster struck. Half an hour before the performance, Toby Fettle turned as white as chalk and sprinted to the jakes. We heard terrible groans coming through the door. Master Pink sent Kit to see what was wrong.

"He has been puking up his guts," Kit reported cheerfully. "And now he says he has the flux."

Master Pink clearly felt no sympathy for Toby. "I warned him not to eat those herrings," he said irritably.

"Now I doubt the foolish boy can act today. You will have to play Philomena instead," he said to Kit. "You know her speeches, don't you?"

"I do," said Kit. "But there is one small difficulty."

"A very small difficulty," Sam agreed mischievously, and he held up Philomena's gown.

Master Pink looked at sturdy Kit, then at the dainty gown, and he struck out violently at the wall. "A pox on you, boy!" he cursed. "What made you grow so stout?"

"Why cannot Robert do it?" grinned Ned. "He is a sweet girlish sort of fellow."

I quickly made a fist at him.

"Do you know the part?" Master Pink asked.

"I think I can manage it," I replied bravely. "If you will all help me."

The other players went into a whirl of activity, handing me Philomena's wig and gown and giving helpful advice on how to act like a girl.

"Well, this is wondrous strange," I whispered to Kit. "I shall be a girl playing a boy who is playing a girl."

"You'll be saving our bacon, Master Robert," Kit hissed in my ear. "That's what you'll be doing. Now don't blink or I shall poke you in the eye." And he began to outline my eyes in black paint.

That afternoon I played Princess Philomena in front of the good people of the town. I trembled with stage fright at first. But Master Pink, playing Saint George, fixed me with such an entranced expression every time I said my lines that I began to be convinced he was really in love with me.

The play was going better than I had dared to hope, when suddenly a wild-haired drunk burst into the tavern yard and started haranguing everyone at the top of his voice. "These ruffians have stolen my pig!" he ranted. "A fine beast, he was, a prince among pigs. Then this band of robbers trooped through the marketplace, and when I went to the sty, the beast had gone. Give me back my pig, you scurvy rascals!" And the man jumped up on the stage and seized Master Pink by the ear.

Master Pink was well accustomed to dealing with this kind of misunderstanding. With a thrilling clash of steel, he drew Saint George's sword and swiftly improvised new lines for England's patron saint. "Sir, I must ask you to unhand me," he said with great dignity. "I have undertaken to rescue a fair maiden from a fearsome dragon and have no choice but to slay anyone who gets in my path! But when my task is done, sir, I promise to help you find the villain who has stolen your most noble pig."

Everyone roared with laughter. The man staggered slightly and let go of Master Pink, looking bewildered.

"Do not heed the drunken fool," a woman shouted out. "He knows not what he is saying."

"I have seen this pig prince and believe me, 'twas no more than a piglet," yelled a witty youth.

"If you ask me, he felt peckish and ate it himself!" suggested someone.

Seeing that the audience was on our side, the land-lord of the Angel firmly led the troublemaker away, and we were able to go on with our play without further interruption. At last it ended in a storm of applause.

"The lad actually blushed when Jasper kissed him at the wedding!" Ned told everyone delightedly.

"You are an actor born, Master Robert," Kit said with a mischievous grin.

For the rest of my time with the players, excitement bubbled up inside me each and every time I went on stage, but the life of a traveling player was not the idyll I'd imagined. We had to tramp from place to place in all weathers, sleeping in woods and fields, and were often damp, cold, and hungry. Nor were we always welcome. Like the man with the missing pig, many country folk believed that players were thieves and ruffians, so if livestock vanished or a precious ring went missing, we automatically got the blame. Some people thought playacting itself was a sin, corrupting those who came to watch. Others feared we brought contagion with us from London, for lately there had been rumors of a new outbreak of plague. In one place, angry villagers actually threatened to burn our cart, and we were forced to flee in the night.

Though it was an adventure, life with the players was not for me. I just wished I knew what was.

We were now but a few miles from my aunt's estate. After our performance in Northampton, we were to travel on to the tavern at Pease Magna. There I would say good-bye to the little band of players. Apart from Kit, Master Pink didn't think it wise for them to accompany me to my aunt's.

"I fear the lady might not be too happy to see her long-lost nephew in the company of crude outlaws," was how he put it, and I had not protested. I was not ashamed of my friends, but I was strangely ashamed at having to tell men who had generously befriended me that I was not Robert Campion after all, but Isabel.

I spent my last night with the players in a hayloft belonging to an inn called the Green Giant. I'd grown used to dropping off to sleep wherever I lay my head, but that night I tossed and turned for hours, listening to my companions' snores and the squeaks of field mice running about inside the walls. Next day I would arrive at my aunt's, and I had no idea what awaited me there.

I had been pretending to myself that I didn't miss my family. I had even managed to persuade myself that none of them cared for me. But suddenly I was over-whelmed with such a longing to see them again that I could scarcely breathe. Not wanting to be heard, I turned my face to the cloak that served as my pillow, and for the first time since I had left home, I sobbed until I thought my heart would break.

9 A Merlin for a Lady

Master Pink generously lent us Delilah so that Kit and I could ride the few miles from Pease Magna to my aunt's estate. The landlord of the tavern had helpfully given us directions.

It was evening by the time we arrived, and everything was bathed in a honey-colored light; the honeysuckle in the hedges, the marsh marigolds in the streams, and the warm-colored stone of the great house nestling in the wooded valley were all touched with a golden glow.

Kit's first sight of Aunt de Vere's estate made him whistle. "You didn't say your aunt lived in a manor house with a moat!"

"I didn't know it myself!" I said.

"And she is a widow, you say?"

"My aunt married three times," I said. "But her husbands all died, and she has no children. Now she lives alone with her ward."

"But your aunt is kind, I hope," Kit said in an anxious voice.

"I have only met her twice. The first time I was but a babe. Then last year she came to my mother's funeral. My father says she is religious and devotes her life to good works."

I sighed. During my sleepless night in the hayloft, I had hopefully pictured my aunt as a second mother, supplying the tenderness and understanding I craved. But now that I was actually here, I found myself contemplating a sterner, more critical version of Aunt Elinor.

Kit patted my back. "Be not so cast down, Master Robert. 'Twill be good for you to taste a little religion after consorting with ungodly folk as we!"

Some servants were out on the green, putting up a maypole for the next day's May Day celebrations. They eyed us suspiciously as we approached, clearly wondering why we were here.

Kit called to them, "I have with me a young relative of your mistress, whom we met on the road and took under our protection."

"Mercy!" gasped someone. "That's never the child that was lost?"

"Peter, fetch the mistress!" a woman said urgently. A rosy little boy went racing toward the house.

I found myself being swept over the footbridge with awestruck villagers pressing on either side. Some touched me fearfully to make sure I was not a spirit child, risen from the grave.

As we reached the other side of the moat, Kit and I gazed around us in astonishment. My aunt's estate was vast and even had its own chapel. There were huge stables and other outbuildings, orchards of fruit trees in blossom, and market gardens planted with herbs and vegetables. A crisscross of paths led to a row of well-kept cottages. Wisps of wood smoke rose from their chimneys, like those innocent drawings of home scribbled by little children.

Before we could reach the great house, a tall fair-haired woman in a plain gray gown hurried around the corner, with the rosy little boy clinging to her hand and two hounds bounding at her heels. "If you are telling stories again, Peter," she was saying, half-joking, half-threatening. Then she saw me standing there, with my cropped hair and my boy's disguise. She took a step forward, her piercing blue eyes searching my face. "Lord bless us," my aunt said quietly. "Isabel is alive."

That night I put on a fresh linen shift and climbed up into a big soft bed with curtains as blue as the sky. It felt astonishing to be clean and still more astonishing to be dressed as a girl again. Olivia, my aunt's young ward, had kindly lent me some clothes until Aunt de Vere's dressmaker could measure me for some new gowns.

I didn't yet know what to make of my aunt. I had sensed that she was profoundly happy to see me, not merely relieved. Yet she had not wept or fussed over me as many women would have done. Nor had she scolded me for causing so much worry and distress. She questioned me about the fate of her servant, and when she heard what had happened, she said simply, "Poor John. He did not deserve such an end. I will pray for his soul." Then my aunt introduced me courteously to Olivia and asked her to take me to my chamber. "I hope you will quickly come to feel at home here," my aunt said briskly. "Tomorrow we will discuss how you are to spend your time here. But for now I shall go and write to your father to let him know you are safe."

I had never met anyone like my Aunt de Vere before. Her bright blue eyes glinted with a keen intelligence, and she radiated such fierce energy and purpose that I felt somewhat intimidated. I sensed that my unusually dynamic aunt lived by a different set of rules than did other women. And I feared that she would soon find me lacking.

Aunt Elinor had told me constantly that I was foolish and undisciplined and that my head was filled with moonshine. What if she was right? Aunt de Vere seemed pleased to see me now, but when she got to know me better, she might be sadly disappointed.

There was a tap at my door. Olivia peeped in. "I wanted to make sure you were really here," she confessed. "I still can't quite believe it."

"I can't quite believe it myself," I said shyly.

Olivia brought her candle into my room. She was slightly older than I was, with a sweet, heart-shaped face, and her manner was engagingly friendly. "As soon as your aunt said you were to come, I made up my mind we would be friends," she said earnestly. "Then, when you disappeared—"

I felt a rush of guilt. "I have given everyone a great deal of trouble."

"No one thinks that," Olivia assured me. "Everyone here is too glad to have you safe. And when your father receives your aunt's letter, your family too will rejoice."

I could not bear to explain how things were between me and my father, so I tried to smile. "My aunt is very kind."

"I will leave you to get your rest," said Olivia. "We are to go a-Maying tomorrow. That's if you are not tired from your travels?"

"Not at all," I assured her. "During my time with the players, I have grown accustomed to doing with very little sleep!"

Olivia's eyes sparkled. "Tomorrow I will make you tell me all your adventures," she said eagerly. "But for now I shall bid you good night." Then she slipped softly out of the door.

But I had never slept alone in my life, and once Olivia had gone, I found myself jumping out of my skin at every sound: the metallic rasp of pheasants, the eerie shriek of owls, and a stealthy padding sound that seemed to be inside the house. *It's coming closer,* I thought. My mouth dried as I heard something scratching at the door to my chamber. A large beast padded to the foot of my bed and stood there, panting in the shadows.

My heart was pounding as I peeped out fearfully between the curtains, and I sighed with relief to see one of my aunt's hounds. He jumped onto my bed and pushed his cold nose into my hand. "You knew I was lonely, didn't you, you dear dog?" I told him gratefully.

And with my aunt's friendly hound for company, I lay down behind my sky blue curtains and gradually drifted into sleep.

At first light, I washed and dressed in a gown of Olivia's, and she and I hurried from the house. It felt magical to be out so early on a May morning—like being back at the dawn of creation, when the world was one big paradise garden, dewy and untouched.

Young serving maids came running from the servants' entrance to join us. We all walked down to the lane and fell in with a troop of village boys and girls. The girls wore crowns of flowers. Together, we went hurrying toward the woods amidst such clouds of may blossom that Olivia said it looked as if the world were having a wedding. I felt a sharp stab of sorrow at

the mention of weddings. *Sabine will be married now,*
I thought wistfully. *I hope she is happy and that she has
forgiven me for ruining her wedding plans.*

But I could not stay sad for long, for at that
moment, a village youth struck up a lively tune on his
fiddle. Some of the other boys had brought pipes and
drums. Everyone began to sing and make merry, and
our walk to the woods became a dance! I saw one of
the girls nudge another one excitedly. " 'Tis the little
mistress," she hissed in a stage whisper. "She was kidnapped by brigands, but traveling players rescued her."

Olivia looked amused. "You are famous," she said
merrily.

With mixed delight and dismay, I recognized Kit
and Sam among the crowd. Kit explained a little shyly
that my aunt had invited the players to perform as part
of the day's celebrations. He and Sam had decided to
come early to help us bring in the May.

"I wanted to see this bold Mistress Isabel for myself,"
Sam said wickedly. He didn't seem annoyed at my
deception so much as faintly admiring. "We all
wondered why Master Robert blushed so prettily when

Jasper embraced him," he joked. "Now we know!"

Sam was soon flirting with the village milkmaids. Olivia went to talk to one of the musicians, and somehow Kit and I fell into step.

We didn't seem to know what to say to each other now that I was a girl again in gown and slippers. And I felt absurdly shy as we walked together, gathering sprays of sweet-scented may blossom from the hedges. Then, when all our pails and baskets were full, we bore them home in triumph, singing May carols as we came.

The May revels went on with feasting, music, archery contests, and dancing around the maypole, now garlanded with spring flowers and colored ribbons. The other players arrived at midday with Delilah's cart and began to set up the stage. At last Ned blew three blasts on a battered horn, signaling the start of the play, and Saint George strode on stage, magnificent in chain mail and leather breeches.

It felt quite peculiar to be watching from the audience, and I found myself anxiously murmuring Philomena's lines under my breath. I was very relieved to see that the audience laughed and cried in all the right places. And when the play ended, they applauded and stamped enthusiastically. My aunt told the players they were welcome to stay the night, but Master Pink said they must press on to Stourbridge.

"Then please accept this purse with my gratitude for your kindness to my niece," said my aunt as she gave an astonished Master Pink a purse jingling with gold and silver crowns. He grew quite emotional and tried to give it back, insisting that my presence in itself had been sufficient reward to the players, but my aunt would not hear of it.

I now had to say good-bye to Kit for the second time. If anything, the second time was more painful than the first. Since our walk together in the greenwood we had become strangely tongue-tied. *All because I have put on this stupid gown*, I thought miserably. I began to be convinced that Kit did not like me nearly so well now that I was Isabel again.

In desperation I called after him, "Farewell! Tell Meg I still have her lucky charm."

He swung round, looking unusually solemn. "'Tis not farewell, mistress. We shall meet again, if God wills it," he called back. And I found myself blushing in confusion, just as I did when Saint George kissed Philomena.

I walked slowly back across the grass, having to remember to hold my skirts out of the dirt. For weeks I had worn doublet and hose, pretending to be a boy. Now I felt as if I were just pretending to be a girl.

Who am I really? I thought anxiously. I was no longer Robert, nor was I that pampered girl who had left London. *I am no one*, I thought, and I felt a sudden pang of loss. From this time on, I would always be a stranger living among strangers.

Then I pictured my aunt's kind, calm face as she said, "Isabel is alive," and I thought, *This is not my home yet, but perhaps one day it may be.* And at that moment Olivia caught me up breathlessly and led me off to see the fireworks.

Next day Olivia was excused from her tasks so that she could show me around the estate. First we visited my aunt's dairy and the brewhouse, and then we went to peep in through the door of the low mews, where my aunt kept many fine hunting birds. It was a beautiful May morning, but inside the mews it seemed to be perpetual dusk. My eyes gradually adjusted to the gloom, and I felt a prickle of pleasure as I made out the silent birds hunched upon their wooden perches. They seemed severe and contemplative in their brooding silence, like monks, or the questing knights of old.

I should have liked to go inside, but a stooped old man came out and told us gruffly that we must not go in the mews without my aunt's permission.

Olivia hurried me off to see the stables and introduced me proudly to her favorite horse. "We can go riding together every morning before lessons," she said merrily.

"Oh, yes, lessons," I sighed.

My aunt had explained that she would be taking charge of my education herself, and I had gloomy visions of adding columns in an account book and having to clean greasy velvet with goose feathers.

I confessed this to Olivia, and she gazed at me with

astonishment. "Didn't your father tell you that your aunt is a learned lady?"

"He said only that she was very religious and good," I told her.

"She is certainly good," said Olivia. "I am not even a relative, yet she took me into her household and treats me like her own child. But your aunt's intellect is as keen as any man's. She is so respected in medical matters that famous London apothecaries write to her for advice."

I shook my head in astonishment. My father had not mentioned this either.

"How will she find time to tutor us, with all her good works?" I asked.

"Your aunt finds time for more than other people think possible," Olivia said, laughing. "I think she has more energy than Her Royal Grace herself!"

After our midday meal, my aunt suggested that I go with her and Olivia to visit the clinic she ran for the villagers. I would have preferred to explore Aunt de Vere's library, but I was afraid to displease her. Privately dreading bad smells, I accompanied Olivia and my aunt to the clinic that adjoined the private chapel. Here villagers waited on benches with their warts and boils, agues or green sickness, fevers or flux to be treated by my aunt. As I feared, the air was heavy with the unpleasant odors of poverty and sickness.

I hung back, wishing I had brought my pomander, but Aunt de Vere said briskly, "Since you are here, Isabel, I shall set you to work." At first I only had to consult the enormous herbal to check the right dosages of a particular remedy. Then, to my horror, my aunt called me over to examine a boy with suppurating boils on his neck. "See if you can identify the problem," she said cheerfully.

I gulped. "There is a great deal of pus oozing out," I said in a small voice.

"Exactly," said my aunt. "And have you noticed that curious stench? 'Tis almost exactly like bad meat?"

I nodded, desperately trying to hide my revulsion.

"Normally I would lance the carbuncles. But they have become so infected that the procedure would do more harm than good. Instead we will apply a poultice to draw forth the evil humors." My aunt asked me to bring her certain herbs from the supply in the clinic storage cupboard. While I nervously measured out the correct quantities of yarrow, horse chestnut, and other healing herbs, she stood over me and explained how to use them to make a healing poultice.

As the afternoon went on, I grew less preoccupied with my own distress and started to feel genuine concern for our patients. I listened attentively as my aunt dispensed her herbal remedies: feverfew for headache or giddiness, comfrey for bruising and to knit broken bones, barberry for antiseptic, and yarrow to stanch bleeding.

One woman had come to plead for an elixir to ward off plague. She had heard the rumors that a new epidemic of the disease had begun in London. Her husband had to drive his cattle to the city, and she was terrified that he might become infected.

"You have no cause to fear," an old woman reassured her. "Plague is sent to punish sinners in the cities, not God-fearing folk such as we."

I wanted to tell her, "My family lives in the city, and they are not sinners. Besides, in the past many good people have died of the plague." But I knew she was really trying to comfort the drover's wife and meant no harm, so I held my tongue. In any case, my aunt had reassured me that the last time she had heard from my father, everyone in the household had been in good health.

I noticed that my aunt did not dismiss the woman's worries but took them seriously, suggesting simple measures such as keeping her house scrupulously clean, changing clothes and bedding regularly, and strewing doorsteps with rue to protect her family against contagion. "And tell your husband he must not handle any coins unless they have first been soaked in vinegar," she advised.

I was filled with admiration for my aunt. I knew she had suffered many losses in her life. Olivia had told me that of my aunt's five infants, none had survived more than a few hours. Yet my aunt devoted her wealth and energy to serving those who were less fortunate.

At last all the patients had been seen, and we went out into the warm afternoon sunshine. My aunt turned to me and said, "Cole informs me that you looked in to see my hawks." She smiled. "Cole is a most vigilant master falconer! No one gets near those precious birds without him knowing. Are you interested in my hunting birds?"

"Oh, yes," I said eagerly.

"If you do not mind rising early, I will introduce you to them properly tomorrow," she suggested.

Olivia at once excused herself with an apologetic smile. "I do not like their smell," she explained.

The next morning, before we had broken our fast, I visited the mews with my aunt.

"We have one young hawk that Cole has raised from a chick," she explained as we crossed the yard. "We have recently begun training her." She gave me a mischievous smile. "It is not usual, I know, for a lady to involve herself with the training of hunting birds, but hawks have always fascinated me."

My aunt softly unlatched the door, and I followed her into the mysterious dusk of the mews. This time I noticed strips of sacking hanging between the crude perches, like banners in a chapel. Unlike Olivia, I did not mind the sharp smell rising from the straw beneath my feet. I was too enthralled by the hawks themselves. At our approach, all the birds simultaneously stirred their feathers, and the mews filled with an eerie rattling sound.

The master falconer came out of the gloom. Aunt de Vere introduced me, and Cole made me a creaky bow, scrutinizing me with the bright impersonal gaze of one of his birds.

"So your niece likes my hawks?" he said gruffly to my aunt.

"She would like to see the young merlin, if that is all right with you." My aunt spoke to Cole not as if he was a servant, but more as if he was an equal whose opinion she valued.

Cole disappeared behind one of the sacking screens. I heard him murmuring soothingly. He emerged with a hooded falcon perched upon his thickly gloved wrist. Little leather straps called *jesses* dangled from the merlin's legs. Cole had attached the jesses to a leash, which was now looped around his glove and finally tied around his little finger, so that the half-trained bird could not fly away in a panic.

Cole softly removed the hood, and suddenly the young merlin was staring back at me with large unblinking eyes. The falcon's brown head and body were softly speckled like an owl's. Its hunched shoulders had a warm rusty coloring, and its tail had irregular bands of cream.

"He looks so severe and noble," I gasped. "Like a knight on a quest!"

My aunt looked amused. "Except that your little feathered knight is actually a lady!" She laughed at my surprise. "Did you not know? The fastest and fiercest hawks are always female." Aunt de Vere reached into a cloth bag at her waist and, as if it was the most normal thing in the world, brought out a dead field mouse! "I took it from one of the traps in the kitchen," she explained in a matter-of-fact voice. She slipped one hand into a leather gauntlet and held out the tiny corpse to the merlin. The young hawk seized the mouse avidly and began to rend and tear at its flesh with cruel-looking talons. But I knew the merlin was not really cruel. Like a cat or a deer, it was simply expressing its God-given nature.

All at once I felt a soundless commotion in the air above me, as a jealous hawk sped toward the merlin like a vengeful arrow. I felt its wing tips brush my cap in passing.

Cole acted quickly. "Take the merlin, if it please you, mistress, or the birds will crab. I will deal with this troublesome gentleman."

My aunt calmly pushed her gloved finger against the merlin's feet so it was forced to step onto her hand or lose its balance, speaking to the bird all the while in a quiet, soothing voice. Meanwhile, Cole captured the angry male hawk and returned it to its perch.

"What does 'crab' mean?" I asked.

"It is hawking language for 'fight,'" my aunt smiled. "As you said yourself, these birds have something in common with questing knights. But we prefer them to keep their ferocity for the hunt, not to get distracted by fighting each other."

"Perhaps it would interest you to see the merlin being trained, little mistress?" Cole suggested shyly. "You'd have to get up betimes. Soon after dawn is best." He gave me a sweet, rather mysterious smile. "A merlin is a fitting hunting bird for a lady, so they say."

"You are honored, Isabel," my aunt told me as we walked back to the house. "I am the only female Cole allows near his birds, and that is purely because I pay his wages!"

"Why is a merlin a fitting bird for a lady?" I asked.

"There is a hierarchy in hunting birds, as in everything else," she said. "You may know that the law forbids a poor man to ape his betters by wearing fine clothes and ornaments?"

I nodded. My aunt was referring to a law known as the "sumptuary law."

"Well, it is the same with birds. Any knave may own a kestrel if he chooses, but only an earl may own a peregrine falcon, and no one but a king may fly a gyrfalcon." My aunt gave me a wry smile. "The English gentry take hawking very seriously, Isabel. Some aristocrats believe that hawking is suited only to men of noble birth, because of the intense self-discipline and patience it demands."

She shot me one of her penetrating looks. "You did not flinch, Isabel, when that angry bird came flying at you. That was bravely done."

"I was not being brave," I said truthfully. "I was awe-struck. The hawk seemed so still and silent, yet he was flying at tremendous speed."

"You are unusually observant," said Aunt de Vere approvingly. "That bird was a kestrel. Kestrels spot their kill from on high, and once they've found it, they plummet in deadly silence like a flash of summer lightning."

"What about merlins?" I asked impulsively. "How do they fly?"

"Our Maker did not design merlins for the dizzy heights," she explained. "A merlin must hunt a little closer to the earth. But she sees a great deal. Rather like you, Isabel," she added, and I heard affection in her voice.

"Is that why men have decided that merlins are suitable for ladies?" I asked. "For I have noticed we are not supposed to soar to the heights, either."

My aunt burst out laughing. "Isabel, shame on you! You are that rare creature, a female who thinks for herself. If you are not careful you will end up like me!"

I had not meant to be outspoken. But my aunt seemed delighted, and though she quickly composed herself, I saw that she thoroughly approved of the way I had spoken my mind.

10 *The Plague Mask*

My life quickly fell into an enjoyable routine. At
the crack of dawn, I watched Aunt de Vere train her
hawks, after which we joined Olivia for lessons. My
aunt was teaching us Greek, Latin, mathematics,
and a little astronomy. To my delight she also told us
wonderful stories, just like Master Hart used to. Two
afternoons a week, I helped in the clinic. Here Olivia
and I learned how to dispense herbal medicines under
my aunt's careful supervision. She taught us about the
importance of the four humors and the use of leeches,
and how certain ailments are affected by the position
of the stars and the phases of the moon.

But by far my favorite part of the day was the time
I spent with the hawks. I found it thrilling to be so
close to such powerful creatures. It was also wonderful

to have Aunt de Vere to myself.

One day my aunt made an astonishing suggestion. "I think you should take over the merlin's training, with Cole's help, of course. You are clearly fascinated by the birds, and you learn quickly."

"You mean I will be able to take her out hunting one day?" I could hardly believe my ears.

My aunt's blue eyes were warm. "I mean she is yours."

I didn't know what to say. Then I asked shyly, "May I give her a name?"

"Of course," smiled my aunt. "Have you a name in mind?"

"Oh, yes," I breathed. "I shall call her Nicolette."

As my aunt said, training a hawk demanded considerable patience and self-discipline. I worked with the merlin each morning, coaxing her to trust me. Cole said that I must increase the length of her leash every time I took her out, so that she became gradually accustomed to flying greater distances. I encouraged Nicolette to fly back to me, first from the door of the mews, then from the mews to the stables, and finally to the other side of the stable yard. Once she had mastered this, we began training her to attack a lure, a stuffed bird of cloth and feathers. This was to encourage and sharpen Nicolette's natural instincts to hunt and kill small birds. Hawks cooperate with humans only if they are hungry, and at the end of each training session, I fed the bird with morsels of raw meat. I had lost all traces of squeamishness and frequently took dead mice out of the traps myself so that Nicolette was sure of a tasty reward.

The outside world seemed far away. London was hazy to me now, like a distant dream. Then one afternoon I heard two gentlemen on the steps of the village church, discussing a friend who had caught the plague in London and sickened so quickly that he died on the journey home. I felt a dim pang of worry, yet I could not really take it in. Although my aunt constantly assured me that there was no mention in my father's letters of any illness, I'd had no direct word from my family since I had come to live in Northamptonshire. I knew Sabine must be married now, and found it impossible to imagine my home without her. I missed all my family and often thought wistfully of Meg when I was alone, but now my life seemed to be here in this peaceful valley.

One day my aunt had to go into Northampton on business and asked me to help Olivia at the clinic. She instructed us to deal only with simple health problems and to tell any patients with more serious symptoms to come again next day.

Unusually, there were few patients that day. First Olivia saw a mother whose little boy had pushed a bean up his nose. I had to hold him still while Olivia carefully extracted it with the help of a mirror and some tweezers.

The next patient was a man shivering violently with an ague. While Olivia was noting down his symptoms, a young woman came in with a sick baby, though with the great hollows under his eyes he looked like a tiny wizened old man. I heard the breath rasping in his lungs as he struggled for air.

"He's been like this for two days," the woman said anxiously. "Will my baby die, little mistress?"

"Of course not! He'll be better in no time," I said confidently. Recently my aunt had treated a local shepherd also suffering from asthma. I remembered that she had prescribed the herb bryony, so I quickly consulted the herbal and gave the woman the recommended dosage. I felt a rush of pride to think that I was on my way to becoming a professional herbalist, just like my aunt. I had actually helped a sick baby all by myself!

Before we closed the clinic, Olivia glanced at the ledger in which we wrote the name of each patient, together with his or her symptoms, the remedy, and the dosage. She looked puzzled. "Did you see this mother and child, Isabel? I'm sure I did not."

"I saw them while you were busy with that man," I said proudly. "Don't worry, I looked up the remedy and dosage in the herbal."

Olivia turned pale. "Isabel, that dosage is for adults. You have given that baby enough to kill him!"

I felt sick with horror. "Do you know where she lives?"

"Yes, it isn't far."

"We'll go on horseback. We may still catch her in time."

I ran to fetch our horses while Olivia quickly found the correct dosage. We galloped frantically along the lanes. Finally we came in sight of a tumbledown hovel. I heard a young child wailing inside. Not bothering to knock, we rushed inside.

"Have you given your baby the remedy?" Olivia demanded.

The woman looked guilty. "Not yet, little mistress, for I could not get the fire to light."

"Oh, thank God—" I began.

"Mistress Isabel has thought of a better remedy for your little boy," Olivia said quickly. "It will work much more swiftly than the first."

"How can I thank you, miss! I've been so worried."

The woman's eyes filled with tears.

I felt deeply ashamed. Olivia had made it seem as if I was the baby's savior, when I had almost cost him his life.

"No harm was done," Olivia comforted me as we rode home. "We need not tell your aunt."

But I couldn't let Olivia cover up my mistake. More than anything else in the world, I wanted to be like my aunt. Over the last few months, I had learned to love as well as respect her, and I sensed that she loved me. I knew I owed it to Aunt de Vere to tell her the truth, though I dreaded what the consequence of my confession might be.

That evening I went to look for my aunt. I found her in the knot garden, enjoying the lingering sunset, and I poured out my story.

"I fear you are disappointed in me, Aunt," I said in a low voice.

She gave me one of her piercing looks. "Yet you came to tell me. Why?"

"Because I would not be able to look you in the eyes. It would always be between us like a shadow."

Aunt de Vere stooped to smell a moss rose with creamy pink-tipped petals. "Isabel, it seems to me that you cannot always tell the difference between your imaginings and real life. You let yourself get carried away by your own heroic notions, and today a child almost died because of that."

I knew my aunt was right. I waited wretchedly for her to say she was sending me away as my father had done.

Her next words astonished me. "We all need dreams, Isabel," my aunt said softly. "Our dreams make us what we are, but we women must always keep our feet on the ground."

I blinked. Aunt de Vere had referred to me as a woman, not a child.

"You must give me your word that you will never make such a mistake again," she said in her calm, quiet voice.

"I—I give you my word, Aunt," I faltered.

She smiled. "Then we need never mention this matter again."

I almost wept with gratitude. I saw that my aunt

trusted me to keep my word, and I made up my mind that from then on, I would do everything in my power to make her proud of me.

Spring turned into summer. Tiny apples and plums began to swell in the orchards. My aunt's stillroom filled with the scent of roses as the women distilled wild rose petals to make the rosewater we used for washing, cooking, and medicinal purposes.

One morning, I rose just before dawn as usual. But I felt strangely agitated as I hurried downstairs to meet my aunt. I was excited but also very scared. Today we were to let Nicolette off the leash for the first time. It seemed a terrifying thing to let her just fly away into the limitless sky, but Cole had explained that there was no other way.

I confided my fears to my aunt as we hurried across to the mews, leaving tracks in the dew. "Suppose she decides she wants to be free forever? Suppose she just flies off and never comes back?"

My aunt gave me one of her wry smiles. "She is a female," she said. "Like all females, she is permitted to be free only within limits. You and Cole have taught her that she must always return home, and so she will."

We set out toward the water meadows, with Nicolette riding proudly on my wrist. She looked calm and alert, her bright eyes registering every flickering leaf and grass blade. I sensed that she was happy just being herself, with the dawn chorus pouring from every tree and the soft morning breeze ruffling her speckled feathers.

Suddenly we heard loud shouts. A young groom came galloping up on a horse. I saw that the beast had been ridden hard, for its coat was covered with lather. The youth was so distressed that he barely remembered to bow to my aunt. "Master Reynolds has sent me to fetch you," he panted out. "Mistress Reynolds became delirious with fever on their return from London, and Master Reynolds fears it is the plague."

I felt a jolt of horror, but my aunt showed no sign of alarm.

"Cole, my friend, we will save this for another day," she said quietly. "Isabel, please run and fetch my bag. We will ride together to Master Reynolds's house."

I hurried to find the bag that my aunt kept stocked

with remedies for just such an emergency, and returned to the stables. I swung myself onto the horse behind my aunt, and we went clattering out of the stable yard.

I told myself that I must not think of my own safety. I should be thinking of poor Master Reynolds and his young wife. Master Reynolds was a highly respected local lawyer. He and his pretty wife had not been married long and had recently moved into a fine house on the edge of Northampton.

"'Twas Master Reynolds's mother who sent for Doctor Cornelius," the groom was babbling. "But the master says the doctor is a thieving charlatan, and he insisted I come and fetch you, mistress."

My aunt gave a philosophical sigh. "Doctor Cornelius will not be pleased to see me, but we will cross that bridge when we come to it."

How does she stay so calm? I wondered, for my palms were sweating with anxiety.

The lawyer ran out to meet us as soon as he heard the horses' approach. He was almost hysterical with worry. "Cornelius is here, but the man refuses to take off his mask to examine her properly. Please come quickly!"

We hurried up the staircase after Master Reynolds. I followed my aunt into the bedchamber and started with fright. A nightmarish figure loomed over the sick woman. In his hideous metal plague mask, Doctor Cornelius looked like a bizarre beaked monster. He evidently believed that his physician's mask, with its inner compartment filled with sweet-scented herbs, would protect him from infection. But I thought it was a wonder his patients didn't die of fright!

Doctor Cornelius was clearly furious to see my aunt. "I must ask you to leave at once, Mistress de Vere, and take your little apprentice with you," he commanded. "This most unfortunate lady has contracted plague!" Booming from inside the mask, the doctor's voice sounded unnaturally hollow. The eerie sound seemed to penetrate Mistress Reynolds's delirium. She began to whimper with distress, tossing to and fro on her pillows. I saw that her face was mottled with fever and her damp hair clung to her forehead.

Perhaps Mistress Reynolds really was suffering from plague. I knew that a high fever was one of the first signs. No one knew for sure just how the plague was spread, but some said it traveled invisibly through the air. It was possible that my aunt and I were breathing it in at this moment.

But my aunt seemed utterly unafraid. "I will leave only if Master Reynolds asks me to, since it is he who sent for me," she pointed out mildly. "Perhaps you could tell us why you are so convinced that his wife has the plague, for I believe you have not actually examined her."

"How dare you challenge my judgment, madam!" the doctor blustered. "Mistress Reynolds needs a physician's skill, not your herbal quackery. I was just about to examine the lady when you burst in."

"Yes, I see you have your physician's cane at the ready," commented my aunt, eying the implement with some scorn.

"Indeed I do, madam! You would not expect me to touch an infected woman with my bare hands!" the doctor scoffed from behind his mask.

Aunt de Vere seemed to be making an effort to control her temper. "If you do not object, I would like to examine your wife, Master Reynolds," she said softly.

Master Reynolds readily gave his consent. Doctor Cornelius stood by fuming as my aunt quickly examined Mistress Reynolds. I noticed that she paid close attention to the condition of her patient's skin, particularly the armpits. At last, Aunt de Vere looked up with a smile. "It is not plague, Master Reynolds, never fear. Your wife has no blisters, and I can find no sign of plague boils forming in her groin or armpit. In my opinion she has a severe quinsy. It is that which is making her delirious."

Doctor Cornelius immediately turned on his heel and went storming out, almost knocking me over in his fury. As he reached the door, he whipped off the mask, and I saw a furious whiskery face underneath. "Pah!" he spat at me. "Someone should teach that woman to know her place!"

But it seemed to me that my aunt had taught Doctor Cornelius his place, because it was he who was forced to leave and my aunt who had stayed.

Aunt de Vere showed me how to bathe our patient with cooling rosewater to bring down her fever. I sponged the lady's burning hot face and limbs as gently as I could. After only half an hour or so, she suddenly opened her eyes and said in an astonished voice, "Why, Mistress de Vere, how come you and little Isabel to be in my chamber?"

Poor Master Reynolds almost wept with relief.

Before we left, my aunt gave him an herbal tincture that she said would help his wife recover more quickly. "Give her twenty drops in barley water four times a day until your wife's symptoms improve," she told Master Reynolds. "And be sure to give her plenty to drink until she is strong enough to take proper nourishment."

"Mistress, I cannot thank you enough," he said warmly.

I was almost light-headed with happiness as Aunt de Vere and I rode back through the town. Mistress Reynolds would soon be well again, and I had helped my aunt restore her to health.

We had taken a different route home, one that led us through the poorer part of town. Dismal tumble-down cottages huddled on either side of the street, with a stinking ditch between them. I caught the quick flicker of a hairless tail as a large rat disappeared into a heap of rotting garbage. Suddenly a shiver went down my spine. The windows of one of the cottages had been boarded up, and someone had painted a dull red cross upon the door. I knew at once that someone within had died of plague.

My aunt's expression was compassionate. "I fear many hundreds will die in our towns and cities before the summer is over. Warm weather and squalor provide the perfect conditions for the infection to thrive."

I felt a pang of fear for my family and quickly felt for the lucky stone that hung around my neck, to reassure myself that it was still there. Perhaps Meg's charm did have genuine protective powers, for since I had been wearing it, I had narrowly avoided being murdered by brigands, and now I had been spared a potentially fatal encounter with the plague. I offered up a silent prayer of thanks, never dreaming that in a few hours I would deliberately choose to expose myself to this virulent disease.

On our return, we found Olivia pacing anxiously,

clearly distressed. She whispered to my aunt and gave her a letter. *That is Sabine's writing,* I thought.

"It is for you, Isabel. I fear you must prepare yourself, my dear," my aunt said gently, "for the messenger told Olivia it was a matter of life or death."

I frantically scanned the pages.

Sabine spent the first few paragraphs apologizing for not writing sooner and saying how she missed me. She said that she and Henry were now living on Henry's country estate, which was but a few miles from my new home, and that they would both be delighted to have me to stay. My sister went on to say that she had received distressing news from London.

Our father is presently overseas on business, leaving Aunt Elinor in sole charge of the household. In his absence, it seems that our aunt's morbid fear of the plague has worked on her nerves. This morning I received word from Master Johnson's wife that my aunt has banished all the servants from the house except for our old nurse. Unfortunately, little Hope has now fallen gravely ill. Mistress Johnson fears that the responsibility

*for nursing her has overwhelmed my aunt, so that she
seems on the brink of nervous collapse. I would go to her,
but I am expecting a child. Because of my condition,
Henry has put his foot down. . . .*

The letter fell from my hand. The plague had never
seemed so real as it did at this moment. My tutor had
once explained that epidemics of plague came in
waves, lying dormant for decades and then erupting
anew. But to me, this nightmarish disease had always
belonged safely to the past, with all those other
ominous events in England's history—wars, religious
persecutions, threats of foreign invasion—events that
older people liked to reminisce about but that had not
touched me personally. But it had come back, here
and now, into my present.

I found myself remembering gruesome details I
would have preferred to forget: once healthy skin
turning blistered and black; giant purple plague boils
oozing pus. I knew this terrible contagion struck with
such supernatural speed that its victims frequently
died within hours of the appearance of the first

symptoms. My baby sister could already be dead.

I was terrified, yet I did not hesitate. "My sister is gravely ill, and my aunt is in no state to care for her. I must go to them," I said.

"You will be taking a terrible risk," my aunt said anxiously. "They say that there is not a single London street that has not been touched by the plague. You know that I would go with you, dear heart, but my patients need me here."

I shook my head. "I have to go. I have no choice." For the first time in my life, my family needed me. I prayed only that I was not too late.

11 *City of Ghosts*

The first thing I noticed was the sound of water.

I had left a London of thundering carts, pealing bells, and raucous voices bawling out their wares. All these competing noises were combined in a vast restless roar, which ebbed and flowed like the sea and ceased only at nightfall.

But now it was broad daylight, and as we rode past Saint John's Priory, down Ely Place, and onward through Saint Bartholomew and Smithfield, I could hear nothing but rushing streams and the busy trickling of brooks and tributaries, peaceful natural sounds previously muffled by the deafening din of London.

Our horse sensed something was amiss and had to be urged onward with threats and kicks. My aunt's manservant tried to appear unconcerned, but I knew he was afraid. And so was I.

Everything reeked of burning. Smoke hung over the city like fog, and there no longer seemed to be any colors anywhere—no vivid washing strung across alleyways to dry, no pots of sweet geraniums on the sills—just muted tones of smoke and ash. Everywhere, doors and shutters were closed, giving the city the appearance of being blind. Then a shock of red leaped from a door, and I heard the servant gasp with fear as he recognized the crude painted cross announcing that people inside had been visited by plague.

Other flickers of red appeared at street corners, where watchmen's fires burned day and night to destroy the infected clothes and possessions of the dead. In the silence I heard the jangle of a solitary handbell and the trundle of wheels. A weary voice called, "Bring out your dead."

The servant said to me, "Don't look, little mistress!"

But I felt the plague cart go by like a deadly breath. I began to think that I had entered the regions of Dante's hell, which I had learned about from Master Hart. The shadowy Londoners we saw disappearing into alleyways were its unhappy spirits.

I saw so many livid red crosses as we rode through Cheapside that I could only marvel that anyone was left alive. In some streets, green tufts of grass had begun to grow up between the cobblestones. A helpless dread crept over me. I became convinced that I would reach home only to find that crude sign scrawled upon our house, too. If the plague could turn a noisy, rumbustious city into this twilight world of ghosts and shadows, how on earth could a nervous gentlewoman, an elderly nurse, and a sickly little girl survive?

We turned into the street where I had lived almost all my life, urging the exhausted horses over the cobbles toward our large three-gabled house.

Even when I stood right in front of the door, I didn't dare believe my eyes. There must be some mistake! My house had been forgotten. Any moment now I would hear that doleful handbell summoning survivors to bring out their dead.

Then our door opened cautiously, and I heard Alice call to my aunt, "Oh, praise be, Mistress Campion! They have returned!"

They are still alive! I thought.

My old nurse came hobbling out to meet us.

"Does my sister still live?" I asked in terror. "Is it true she has the plague?"

Alice pressed her hands to her mouth. "No, no, my honey. The contagion passed her by. But she is very near death and no longer knows who we are."

"Take me to her!" I pleaded.

I followed my nurse into the back parlor, where a little bed had been made by the fire for Hope. My aunt sat at her bedside, seeming older than I remembered. I saw at once that my baby sister's life hung by the slenderest thread. She plucked feebly at the sheet in her delirium.

"I fear the little thing will not live through the night," my aunt whispered to me. "No matter what anyone says, I know 'tis plague, and soon we shall all be dead." And to my dismay, my father's sister began to cry, with racking dry sobs. I had never seen my aunt weep. She had bitterly endured all of life's disappointments and insisted that we do the same. But the terror of the plague, together with my sister's illness, had finally broken her.

The long journey had exhausted me, and the sights and smells of the plague-stricken city played upon my nerves. More than anything I longed to wash away the deadly smoke and dust in a hot tub of sweetly scented water, followed by a bowl of broth and a long night's sleep. But I saw that only one person could restore my home to health and harmony now, and it was me.

I spoke roughly to my aunt, trying to bring her out of her hysteria. "You are wrong, Aunt Elinor," I said fiercely. "My sister does *not* have plague." I lifted up the covers and showed her Hope's flushed but otherwise flawless skin. "There are no blisters, no discoloring of the skin, and no boils. She has a grave infection, but she does not have plague."

But my aunt seemed unable to understand what I was saying. "You go and rest, Aunt," I said more gently. "It is my turn to sit with Hope now. I will bathe her face and try to bring down her fever."

"I have sponged the little thing morn and night," said my aunt brokenly. "'Tis to no avail."

"Yes, but Aunt de Vere's flower water has special

cooling properties," I said in a firm voice. I knew that a nurse must always seem cheerful and confident. Aunt de Vere said that an atmosphere of doom and despair easily communicates itself to sick children when they are delirious.

"I need warm water to wash my hands," I told Alice. "I cannot touch my sister in this grimy state."

The night that followed was the longest of my life. My small sister had become dangerously weak, and I dared not leave her side. I bathed her face and body repeatedly with Aunt de Vere's cooling flower water, and I burned scented herbs to clear the infection from the room as my aunt had taught me. Then I took my sister on my lap and spooned minute quantities of thin porridge into her mouth, as Alice herself had done when Hope was a feeble newborn babe.

"Come, little one," I coaxed. "Alice prophesies you are to live to the great age of one hundred and four and have ten great hulking sons, so eat your porridge and get well and strong."

Almost no porridge went into Hope's mouth, but still I praised her and wiped her face and said she would begin to get well now that she had taken a little nourishment.

It was now past midnight. I set a watch light on the hearth and prepared to sit with my sister through the night. Alice loyally stayed with me, but she was worn out from days of worry and soon fell into an uneasy doze.

My eyelids felt as heavy as lead, but I refused to let them close. I talked to Hope, coaxing forth the tiny spark of life force that I knew persisted inside her.

I sang her lullabies and told her stories about all we would do when she was better. "We will travel in a fine coach to see Aunt de Vere, and I'll take you to see the woolly lambs that look just like the picture in your hornbook, where it says 'L is for Lamb.' And our aunt's cook will let you make gingerbread husbands, for she is not bad tempered like Joan. She will give you five fat raisins for buttons, and you can put them on all by yourself."

And I went on spinning dreams of a future in which my little sister was rosy and full of mischief, carefully counting out raisin buttons for a comical little man made out of dough.

At last I heard a bird give a brief twitter of surprise, and soon other birds began to sing. I looked at my sister lying quietly now in the muted light of dawn, with her small, cool hand resting in mine. And I realized that it was morning and she was living still.

A few days later, I left my little sister in Alice's care and hurried into Cheapside to do some errands. I needed some silken thread. I was trying to persuade Aunt Elinor to sew Hope a new gown out of a pretty remnant of rose-colored silk. I believed it would help my aunt's nerves to have something practical to do.

After I had bought my thread from the mercer's, I went to the apothecary for frankincense and myrrh, for I had learned from Aunt de Vere how to use them to prevent plague.

I walked past the lace maker's where I had seen the fire-eater entertain the Christmas crowd last winter. There were no fire-eaters now, no street musicians or

stilt walkers or men selling sugar pigs on trays. The few
stalls sold basic necessities—dried beans, salted fish,
and bundles of kindling. The streets were almost
deserted, and those who ventured out kept to the
middle of the street, to avoid brushing against walls
that might be infected with the plague.

To my surprise an old scholar had set up a bookstall
on the pavement. I was amused to see a battered
copy of the traveler's tales my brother used to scare
me with when we were young. I would have liked to
flick through its pages, to find the picture of those
unnatural beings whose heads grew beneath their
arms, but I was afraid the book might harbor the
plague, too. Suddenly a voice behind me said softly,
"Master Robert?"

I spun round. "Kit?"

We clutched each other's hands like frightened
children. Then I saw the look in his eyes and was
afraid to ask my next question.

"She died, Isabel," he said bluntly. "My sister died.
She went to nurse a dying woman next door. Meg
said she had no choice, for when the poor woman's

cowardly lummox of a husband saw her plague sores, he ran off and left her with all her little children. Meg said she wouldn't leave a litter of puppies to die as he had done. The woman died, so by law their house had to be shut up for six weeks. The city watch came and nailed up the shutters with Meg and the woman's little children inside. The watchmen brought them food each day, but by then they too had the disease, may their souls rest in peace."

I was so distressed I couldn't speak.

"You are shocked, mistress," he said with pity. "I am sorry. 'Twas only last week it happened, and if I did not blurt it out roughly, I could not tell it at all."

I tried to tell myself that Meg was gone forever, but I could not really take it in. Then my thoughts flashed to my baby sister. I had been away from home for almost an hour. Suppose she had become worse in my absence. I should not have stayed away so long!

"Kit, forgive me, but I must go home! My little sister is very ill." I saw his stricken face and said hastily, "It is not plague, but she came close to death. She is still too weak to speak to us. Can I come and find you when things are better?"

"Nay, I will come to find you, mistress Isabel," he said softly. "If God wills and we are both spared, I promise I will come to find you."

I flew home and found Hope lying so still that she could have been a baby angel carved from marble. I touched her hand fearfully, and it was warm. The relief was too much and I burst into tears.

"What is wrong?" asked Alice in dismay.

"Meg," I sobbed out. "Meg is dead."

"Oh, no," said Alice in distress. "Not that sweet child."

All that day and the days that followed, my mind refused to believe it. How could saucy, rosy-cheeked Meg be dead and my frail little sister alive? It was a mystery too great to grasp, and I kept myself busy so that I had no time to think.

I started to clean our house from top to bottom, for it had been sadly neglected. My aunt was still in a nervous state and Alice was no longer strong, so I had to do it alone. I swept and scrubbed the flagstones. I polished furniture and oak paneling with beeswax until they gleamed. I strewed floors with fresh rushes mixed with rosemary and rue. I stripped sheets from the beds and boiled them in a cauldron and hung them out to dry. Then I walked to the market, where I bought marrowbones and dried beans and such vegetables as were available, and I took these ingredients back home and prepared simple soups and pottages to keep up our strength.

"You must take care, Isabel," my aunt pleaded. "What if you get ill next? What will we do then?"

I had begun to realize that any attempt to reassure my aunt only made her more panic-stricken than ever, so I decided to speak plainly. "Aunt, I am wild and stubborn, as you have often told me. And I am not yet very ladylike, though my Aunt de Vere tells me I am improving. But I am as strong as an ox, and it is my intention to make sure we all survive."

Aunt Elinor gasped and her mouth tightened like a purse string, but as she absorbed my words, I saw something change behind her eyes, and she said quietly, "Then I will help you, Isabel."

That evening I sat up with Alice, singing lullabies

to my sister. On impulse I took down our mother's lute and carefully tuned its strings.

"This belonged to our lady mother, sweeting," I told Hope. "And this is a song she loved to sing."

I began to play. And as I sang I thought of Meg, who would never sing again in this world, and of her brother Kit, who had promised to come and find me if we were both spared.

Toward the end of the song I heard a footstep in the hall. The parlor door opened and someone came to stand behind me.

I faltered, but my father's voice pleaded, "Don't stop." And I felt his hand upon my shoulder. I tried to continue, but my throat was suddenly choked with tears, and I thought I could not go on.

Suddenly I heard Hope's sheet rustle and an unsteady little voice joined mine. "Lullay, lullay, lullay!"

My little sister was sitting up in her shift and nightcap, singing as merrily as a blackbird! She held up her fingers. "Buttons!" she said imperiously. "Five buttons and I do them all myself!"

Alice and I exchanged awed glances.

"Lord bless us," my nurse said in wonder. "Our little angel has come back!"

My father's arm came around me. "Yes," he said huskily. "Lord bless us, our angel has come back."

12 *The Limitless Sky*

The first rays of light glittered in my eyelashes and
I woke, hearing the familiar din of hooves and cart
wheels below my window. I quickly slipped on my
clothes, feeling the irresistible pull to be out of doors.
I slept little these days and had almost no time to
myself, yet I was rarely tired. In fact, I was glowing
with health. I had noticed the same phenomenon in
other plague survivors. We knew how easily life could
be snatched away and refused to squander our brief,
precious time on earth.

I stole downstairs and slipped out into the pearly
morning. Order was gradually being restored to the
household. My father had hired a new cook and maid.
Our gardener was to return today. The unkempt shrubs
and flowerbeds would be pruned and tidied, until they

once more acquired the formal perfection of Aunt Elinor's embroidery.

But today, with rampant blackberries and little mushrooms sprouting among the grass, our garden had an unruly fruitfulness. I wistfully remembered the beautiful countryside around my aunt's estate. I wondered if Cole had flown my merlin without me, and if she had come back to him, or if she had chosen to fly on forever through the limitless sky.

My breath suddenly caught in my throat. I noticed a waterfall of silky crimson roses, my mother's favorite flowers. They normally flowered but once in early summer. This second autumn flowering was like a small miracle. Impulsively, I began to pick the blooms, carefully snapping the thorny stems. I breathed in their sweet scent, and with every breath I thought, *I am alive, I am alive, I am alive.* And I could not help being glad, even though so many others had died that their names would never be written, except in the book of heaven.

When my arms were full of flowers, I took them into the house. I laid half my flowers down in the scullery, then carried the rest up to the schoolroom in memory of poor Master Hart, who had perished cruelly in the plague, along with all his family. I had come across my tutor's precious note-book while I was tidying the schoolroom. It had gotten mixed in with the school-books and put away on the shelves.

I set the vivid blooms upon the hearthstone, remembering how happy my tutor had been to warm himself by Meg's little fire, and I took his note-book with all its unfinished poems and plays and put it beside the flowers. I wanted to believe that my tutor was looking down at me from paradise. I wanted him to know that I would remember his kindness always.

My father spoke from the doorway. "I have come to a decision, Isabel."

He sounded so strange, I thought I had done something wrong. "What do you mean, sir?" I asked him nervously. "If I have displeased you—"

He began to pace along the polished floorboards. "Displeased me," he echoed incredulously. "How could I be displeased with you, Isabel? Your little sister is now in good health. Your aunt has recovered her spirits, and the household is running smoothly."

"I am glad, sir," I said. "But I don't understand—"

"I want you to go back to Northampton to finish your education," my father said in the same brusque voice. But I saw that he was close to tears. "I promise this is no banishment, Isabel. Your aunt and I will bring Hope to Northamptonshire to see you and Sabine whenever possible. I would prefer to keep you here, but that would be wrong."

I stared at him in astonishment. My heart began to beat in my throat. Had I heard right? Was it really possible that my father was setting me free to live as I pleased?

"Your Aunt de Vere is a wise woman," my father said. "It is obvious that you have profited greatly from her guidance." He dropped his voice in awe. "Did you know that male apothecaries write asking for her advice?"

He looked so comically astonished that I was forced to bite my lip, and he said suspiciously, "Are you laughing, Isabel? Are you being impertinent, young lady?" He began to laugh and folded me in his arms, still laughing, and I smelled the dear familiar scent of nutmeg and cinnamon. "I should have written to you," he said in a muffled voice. "But I could not forgive myself for sending you away. Then you came home again and saved us all." I could feel my father struggling for composure. "Your mother would have been so proud of you. I am so proud of you."

He released me from his embrace. "Come break your fast with me, my sweeting, for I must do without your impertinent presence soon enough."

But I told him I would come in a little while. First there was something I had to do.

I put on my cloak and I carried the rest of the roses down to the river. For some moments, I stood watching boats and barges ply back and forth, and I listened to the familiar ferryman's bellow of "Westward ho!" and the plaintive cry of gulls.

Then I went down to the water's edge and tossed my flowers one by one into the Thames. They began drifting slowly downstream, jewel-bright against the filthy water. I found myself remembering the night Meg and I saw the magical barge floating through the dusk. I had still been a child then, full of wild and foolish dreams. Yet impossibly, some of my dreams were now coming true.

I fingered Meg's lucky charm and smiled.

"I am free, Meg," I whispered. "As free as a merlin in the sky."

The End

Then and Now ♦ A Girl's Life

E N G L A N D

Even at age 12, before she became queen, Elizabeth wore jewels and fine gowns that showed her position in society.

I sabel lived in an exciting time. After many years of strife, Queen Elizabeth brought peace and prosperity to England. During her long reign (1558–1603), known as the *Elizabethan Age*, people turned their attention to art, music, literature, and philosophy. It was one of the most creative periods in human history. That creativity was apparent, in part, in the elaborate dress of the Elizabethan nobility and upper classes.

Queen Elizabeth herself set many of the fashion standards. Her fascination with fashion wasn't just vanity—she dressed to impress. She wore huge gowns, rich fabrics, and expensive jewels that indicated the wealth of England—and her own power as ruler.

The huge gowns worn by Elizabethan women and girls like Isabel required special underclothes. A wheel-shaped *farthingale* of wire or whalebone held the skirt out horizontally at the waist and allowed it to fall straight to the ground, and a tight-fitting, stiff corset flattened the stomach.

farthingales

Over these went a *bodice*, or top, and a *kirtle*, or underskirt. Last came the gown, which was sometimes split in the front to show the decorative kirtle underneath. Isabel also attached sleeves and a *ruff* to her bodice. Both men and women wore ruffs, starched material that stuck out in a circle around the neck. Finally, Isabel fastened a chainlike *girdle* around her waist. From it hung keys, a mirror, and a container called a *pomander* filled with herbs to ward off the "bad air" that Elizabethans believed caused disease.

The sixteenth century was a time of exploration and trade. England was one of the top trading nations, and merchants became wealthy buying and selling goods from around the world. Isabel's father traded in spices like pepper and cinnamon, which people used to disguise the taste of spoiled meat.

Elizabethan clothes made of fancy fabrics with large ruffs were anything but practical, but they clearly set a large, wealthy family like this apart from manual laborers.

Many merchants and their families lived in London, the center of business as well as government. Isabel lived in a fine house in the fashionable East End, fronting the River Thames. Many of London's streets were lined with stalls that sold both local goods and such exotic items as live peacocks and apes. The streets were badly paved and crowded, so many people used the Thames to get around the city. The only other way across the river was over London Bridge, where one passed shops and houses—and even the heads of executed traitors stuck on poles to rot.

London's streets were narrow, dark, and filthy.

People dumped garbage, including human waste, right into the street, and rats were everywhere. It was a perfect breeding ground for diseases, the worst of which was the *plague*. The plague was spread through the air and by the bites of rat fleas. Victims developed red boils and sometimes died within a day. Outbreaks usually occurred every two to three years. Doctors tried all sorts of cures, including piercing the boils, bloodletting, and herbal remedies. But few people survived the plague. One outbreak in 1563 killed 20,000 people in London alone—more than one-fifth of the city's population.

Yet, for all its squalor, Elizabethan London was an exciting place. People flocked to the theaters to see plays by new playwrights like William Shakespeare. Londoners of all classes could leave behind the

Doctors tried to protect themselves from catching the plague by wearing masks like this. The beak was packed with strong-smelling herbs. The poker was put in a fire and then used to pierce a patient's boils.

A production of Shakespeare's play, **A Midsummer Night's Dream**, *at London's Globe Theatre*

overcrowded streets of London and enter a marvelous world of sword fights, romance, clowns, ghosts, and witches.

By the time Queen Elizabeth died in 1603, England had become a leader in world trade and colonization, and English literature, customs, and language had spread throughout the world.

Today, English life is much like life in the United States. English girls see many of the same movies and TV shows that are shown in America, and they listen to much of the same music.

English children start school at age five but can leave school at age sixteen. Most schoolchildren in England wear uniforms. Schools that may have been established in Isabel's time now have computers, and students do projects and stay in touch with friends on-line. Many girls play field hockey at school, while soccer, the most popular sport in England, is played mainly by boys.

England is again ruled by an Elizabeth. Other English women have held positions of power as well, such as Margaret Thatcher, a former prime minister of England.

English schoolgirls today

Although Isabel never would have imagined it in 1592, today English is a global language, spoken by more people in more places than any language in

history, and Shakespeare is the best-known, most widely read writer ever. The rich cultural legacy of the Elizabethans lives on in England and around the world.

Some of the jewels in Queen Elizabeth II's Imperial State Crown were worn 400 years ago by the first Queen Elizabeth.

Author's Note

I fell in love with the Elizabethans as a child.
To me the Tudors *were* history. While I was researching
Taking Wing, I reread all the children's historical novels
that had so enchanted me. I was partly looking for
those juicy details of daily life in sixteenth-century
England, but, more importantly, I was after the
exuberant Elizabethan atmosphere that had captured
my heart as a child.

When I began Isabel Campion's story, I happened
to be renting an old sixteenth-century cottage. This
made it easy to picture Isabel rushing downstairs, her
shoes slipping on the polished oak. And thanks to one
winter power failure, I had no difficulty imagining the
icy cold of the sheets when she jumps into bed on
Christmas Eve!

I am fortunate to live where there are a large number
of unspoiled Elizabethan houses, some of which are
open to the public. Kentwell Hall actually stages
historical reconstructions, in which trained volunteers
take over the house and live and work as Elizabethans.

One hot summer's day I explored this ancient moated estate with its cottages, farm, and gardens. We twenty-first-century visitors were encouraged to question the sixteenth-century inhabitants as they went about their tasks, and they would answer in perfect Elizabethan English. I drew on these experiences for Aunt de Vere's country estate.

I also visited the Globe Theatre in London. This reconstruction of the original Shakespearean play-house resembles a giant beehive from the outside, with its authentic thatch of golden reeds. But when I walked through the playhouse door and saw the stage with its "heaven" and "hell," and above all, the *colors*, I believed, just for an instant, that I had traveled back in time. I was able to use my emotions and sensations for Isabel when she joins the excitable crowd at the Rose and is so enthralled by a performance of one of Will Shakespeare's first plays.

Annie Dalton